Rachel Renée Russell

DORK diaries

Dear Dork

SIMON AND SCHUSTER

This edition published 2016
First published in Great Britain in 2012 by Simon and Schuster UK Ltd
A CBS COMPANY

First published in the USA in 2012 as *Dork Diaries 5: Tales from a Not-So-Smart
Misss Know-It-All*, by Aladdin, an imprint of Simon & Schuster Children's Publishing Division.

5 7 9 10 8 6

Simon & Schuster UK Ltd
1st Floor,
222 Gray's Inn Road
London WC1X 8HB

Simon & Schuster Australia, Sydney
Simon & Schuster India, New Delhi

A CIP catalogue record for this book is
available from the British Library.

PB ISBN: 978-1-47114-476-9
eBook ISBN: 978-0-85707-937-4

Printed and bound by CPI Group (UK) Ltd, Croydon, CR0 4YY

MIX
Paper from
responsible sources
FSC® C020471
www.fsc.org

Simon & Schuster UK Ltd are committed to sourcing paper
that is made from wood grown in sustainable forests and support the Forest
Stewardship Council, the leading international forest certification organisation.
Our books displaying the FSC logo are printed on FSC certified paper.

www.simonandschuster.co.uk
www.simonandschuster.com.au

www.dorkdiaries.co.uk

To my wonderful sisters and BFFs,
Damita and Kimberly.
Thank you for being my real-life
Chloe and Zoey! I'm proud (and very
lucky) to be your big sister.

ACKNOWLEDGMENTS

To all my Dork Diaries fans — thank you for loving this book series as much as I do. The real Nikki Maxwell is actually YOU! Stay sweet and smart and always remember to let your inner DORK shine through.

Liesa Abrams, the nicest, coolest, dorkiest (is that a word?) editor in the entire world. No matter how crazy things get, you're forever the calm voice of reason and a bright ray of sunshine. I ALWAYS look forward to working with you (and your two inner tweens). You're an author's dream!

Lisa Vega, my tireless and supertalented art director. You never cease to amaze me with your snazzy layouts and dorkalicious covers. And I STILL love your ice skates. Nikki Maxwell says she would LOVE to be your summer student intern ☺!

Mara Anastas, Carolyn Swerdloff, Matt Pantoliano, Katherine Devendorf, Paul Crichton, Fiona Simpson,

Bethany Buck, Alyson Heller, Lauren Forte, Karin Paprocki, Julie Christopher, Lucille Rettino, Mary Marotta and the entire sales team, and everyone at Aladdin/Simon & Schuster. Thank you for making this series the huge success that it is. What you have accomplished is quite mind-blowing.

Daniel Lazar, my awesome agent at Writers House, who NEVER sleeps! Thank you for going above and beyond your duties at every turn. I adore your wicked sense of humour and endless enthusiasm for all things dorky. To put it simply . . . You ROCK! Also, a special thank-you to Torie for keeping us superorganized and sending me fabulous mail.

Maja Nikolic, Cecilia de la Campa and Angharad Kowal, my foreign rights agents at Writers House, for making Dork Diaries books available to children across the globe. I say "thank you" in thirty-two languages (so far)!

Nikki Russell, my supertalented assistant artist, and Erin Russell, my supertalented assistant writer. I really cherish the time we all spend together creating our wacky Dork Diaries world. You make writing these books so much FUN that it almost doesn't seem like work. Hugs, kisses and lots of love from Mom!

Sydney James, Cori James, Presli James, Arianna Robinson and Mikayla Robinson, my nieces, for being brutal critique partners and willing to work for a weekend-long pyjama party with endless junk food.

WEDNESDAY, JANUARY 1

OMG! I CANNOT believe I'm actually going to go through with this!

It's supposed to be just a little prank. But I have to admit, I'm a little worried. I really need to think about the consequences of my actions.

Because if something goes wrong, there's a chance SOMEONE could actually end up . . . DEAD!

YES, that's correct. DEAD ☹!!

Namely . . . ME! Because if my parents find out about this stupid stunt I'm planning to pull, they're going to KILL me!

It all started when Chloe, Zoey and I decided to have a sleepover during our winter break from school.

We excitedly counted down the seconds to midnight . . . "TEN . . . NINE . . . EIGHT . . .

SEVEN . . . SIX . . . FIVE . . . FOUR . . .
THREE . . . TWO . . . ONE . . ."

HAPPY NEW YEAR!!!

CHLOE, ZOEY AND I CELEBRATE!!

I was really looking forward to a brand-new year. Mainly because last year was filled with SO much drama.

What better way to start things off than with me and my two BFFs having a WILD and CRAZY New Year's Eve pyjama party at Zoey's house?

We pigged out on pizza, double-chocolate cupcakes, M&M's and ice-cream sundaes, and then washed it all down with soda.

Soon we were giggling hysterically and bouncing off the walls from a major sugar buzz.

We were having WAAAY too much FUN painting our nails funky colours and playing TRUTH OR DARE to watch some lame disco-ball thingy drop in Times Square on TV.

"Zoey! Truth or dare?" Chloe asked, locking her eyes on Zoey with an eager grin.

"Truth!" she answered.

CHLOE, ZOEY AND ME, EATING JUNK FOOD
AND PLAYING TRUTH OR DARE

"I have a really good one!" Chloe squealed. "It's

SOOO romantic and from my FAVE book! Okay, who would you rather kiss, Deadly Doodle Dude or Hunk Finn?!"

"Oh! That's easy!" Zoey giggled. "I pick Hunk Finn. He's the sensitive artist type and supercute."

"Yeah, but Deadly Doodle Dude is so . . . morbidly . . . beautiful and intensely . . . doodley," Chloe gushed.

That's when I almost choked on my pizza.

I know my BFF is a hopeless romantic, and I love her to death. But sometimes I worry that her TEETH might be BRIGHTER than SHE is.

Crushing on a DOODLEY guy is just so . . . WRONG!

I mean, is that even a REAL word?!

If I was going to create the perfect guy, he would be KIND, have a good sense of HUMOUR, and be adorably CUTE (just like my crush, Brandon). . .

ME, MIXING UP THE INGREDIENTS TO MAKE
MY DREAM GUY

"Your turn, Nikki," Zoey said, and turned to me. "Truth or dare?"

"Oooh! I have a really good one!" Chloe exclaimed.

A wicked grin spread across her face as she whispered in Zoey's ear.

Zoey's eyes got as big as saucers. "OMG, Chloe! Nikki is going to DIE if we ask her that!" she shrieked through her giggles.

I scrunched up my face and nervously chewed my lip.

Answering a truth about a fictional guy was fun and exciting.

But answering one about a REAL guy could be totally EMBARRASSING.

And I was hoping to AVOID discussing ONE guy in particular, if you know what I mean.

Which meant I didn't have a choice.

"DARE! Nobody's been brave enough to try a dare, so I'll do one. Give me your hardest!" I challenged Zoey.

She tapped her chin, in deep thought.

Then suddenly a sly smirk appeared on her face. "Are you SURE about that, Nikki? Requesting a truth might be A LOT easier."

"Or maybe NOT!" Chloe said smugly.

"Yes, I'm sure. DARE!" I blurted. "Bring it!"

Sometimes I really wish my brain worked faster than my big, fat mouth.

Because it was quite obvious that Chloe and Zoey were up to some mischievous, evil-genius stuff!

But there was just NO WAY I was going to voluntarily SPILL MY GUTS about Brandon in a game.

Until I heard Zoey's dare. . .

OKAY, DARE! NIKKI, I DARE YOU TO SNEAK OVER TO MACKENZIE'S AND TOILET-PAPER HER HOUSE!

I just stared at Zoey and gasped. I couldn't believe my ears.

"OMG!" Chloe exclaimed. "That's so dangerous and

9

sneaky . . . and totally the BEST dare ever!! You GOTTA do it, Nikki!"

I immediately broke into a cold sweat.

"I d-don't know, guys!" I stammered. "I mean, what if I get caught?! I could get in really big trouble! I guess I'm just a big . . . CHICKEN! Sorry to ruin all of the fun."

"Don't feel bad, Nikki. I gave you a supercrazy dare. Only the CCP (Cute, Cool & Popular) kids do stuff like that. Chloe and I are chickens too!" Zoey admitted.

"I KNOW that's right! Buck! Buck! Buck-aah!" Chloe clucked.

I think Chloe and Zoey said those things just to make ME feel better about NOT doing that dare. They're definitely the BEST friends EVER!

To vent our frustration, we played the "Chicken Dance" song and danced and clucked for nine minutes. . .

CHLOE

ME

ZOEY

CHICKENS "R" US

Afterwards, we just sat there staring at each other, wishing our lives were a lot more — I don't know — EXCITING or something.

It was strange because the more I thought about all of the mean stuff MacKenzie had done to us, the more TICKED OFF I got.

There's only so much public humiliation, vicious

teasing, malicious gossip, ruthless sabotage and mean-girl backstabbing that a person can take.

I'd had quite enough of people who went out of their way to make my life totally miserable.

"People" being snobby, shallow, evil girls like, um . . . MACKENZIE HOLLISTER!!

Calling her a "mean girl" is an understatement. She's a DOBERMAN in lip gloss and designer jeans. And for some reason, she HATES MY GUTS!

MacKenzie having to clean up a few rolls of toilet paper is NOTHING compared to the very long list of horribly rotten things she's done to US.

And she's hurt other people too. It was HER fault Brandon almost moved to Florida.

"You know what, guys? I'm STILL pretty angry about MacKenzie locking us in that storage closet right before we were supposed to skate in the *Holiday on Ice* show!" I fumed.

"Yeah! If she'd had her way, we'd still be in there!" Chloe griped. "Until someone found our skeletons!"

ME, CHLOE AND ZOEY,
NOT LOOKING VERY CUTE AFTER BEING
LOCKED IN THAT STORAGE CLOSET FOR
THREE VERY LONG YEARS!!

"You're right! And THAT was the last straw! I've changed my mind about the dare. I'm going to do it! But only if you guys come with me," I announced.

"We've got your back, girlfriend!" Zoey said. "This isn't a dare anymore! It's PAYBACK! I'll get the toilet paper!"

So right now I'm locked in Zoey's bathroom, writing all of this in my diary.

And instead of doing the sleeping part of our sleepover, we're secretly planning the Great Toilet Paper Caper.

The good news is Miss Thang (also known as MacKenzie) is FINALLY going to get just what SHE deserves ☺!!

The BAD news is IF my parents ever find out about this, I'M going to be DEAD MEAT!

I can't believe it's only thirty-seven minutes into the new year and I'm already FREAKING OUT.

One thing is very clear.

THIS year is going to have WAAAAAAY more DRAMA than LAST year.

☹!!

Have you ever had a REALLY bad feeling about something?

And inside your head a little voice is screaming, "NOOOOOOOO! Stop! Don't do it!"

Well, that little voice was warning ME that our Great Toilet Paper Caper was going to be a complete and utter

DISASTER!!

But did I listen? Of course not!

Although, I have to admit, part of me wanted to just call the whole thing off.

Sneaking out into the cold, dark night to wreak havoc on the world sounded exciting. But we could have had just as much fun staying inside doing all of the normal sleepover stuff.

You know, stuff like . . .

Crawling into my warm and cozy sleeping bag and PRETENDING to be asleep.

While my BFFs giggle uncontrollably and pour water on my hand to try and make me pee my pants.

GIGGLE, GIGGLE!!

GIGGLE, GIGGLE!!

GIGGLE, GIGGLE!!

ME, PRETENDING TO BE ASLEEP

17

Stealing Chloe's overnight bag and raiding Zoey's underwear drawer while they're both busy brushing their teeth.

Then secretly stuffing everything in the freezer.

ME, SECRETLY STUFFING CHLOE'S AND ZOEY'S CLOTHES IN THE FREEZER

Taking turns SCARING ourselves to death by telling superSPOOKY stories in the dark by flashlight.

... THEN THE GHOST FLOATED ACROSS THE ROOM, MOANING, "ZOEY!! NIKKI!!"

But another part of me — a very dark and primitive side—wanted DESPERATELY to get even with MacKenzie.

The thought of being a teen rebel with a cause seemed so COOL. At the time, anyway.

Although I'd been to MacKenzie's house before, purely by accident (OMG! THAT'S a long and gut-wrenching story!), I didn't realise she lived only a few doors down from Zoey.

I felt a little better about the whole thing knowing we didn't have to walk very far in the dark.

Zoey and I found torches and gathered up rolls of toilet paper.

But Chloe was no help whatsoever.

She just sat in front of the mirror humming "Girls Just Want to Have Fun" while making-up her face to look like a bunny.

"Um . . . Chloe. . ." I gawked at her in confusion. "You realise we're not going to a costume party, right?"

"Hey! I know what I'm doing," she assured me. "If we get caught, do you think the cops will arrest an adorable little bunny and throw her in jail? Of course not! But I'll definitely come and visit you and Zoey in the slammer."

Okay! NOW I was starting to get a little worried.

As we trudged through the snow to MacKenzie's house, it was pitch-dark and eerily quiet. All we could hear was the crunching of the snow underfoot and our heavy breathing.

I had to resist the urge to turn around and run screaming back to my warm and safe sleeping bag.

Finally we reached MacKenzie's house, and it was just like I had remembered.

GINORMOUS!!

Suddenly my stomach felt superqueasy.

Only, I didn't know if it was all the junk food I'd eaten earlier that night, OR the fact that I was very close to finally getting a meet-'n'-greet with some of my favourite rap artists who were doing time in prison.

As a fellow INMATE ☺!! YIKES!!

"Come on! Let's get this done before somebody sees us," I whisper-shouted.

Zoey took six rolls of toilet paper out of her backpack and tossed them to Chloe and me.

Chloe and Zoey ran towards a huge tree on the left, and I ran towards one on the right.

Then we frantically tossed the toilet paper over the branches until the two trees looked like towering six-metre mummies.

OMG! It was such a RUSH!!

ZOEY

CHLOE

24

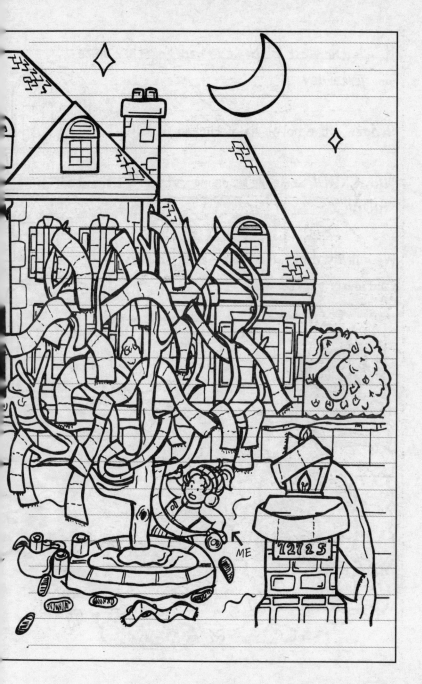

ME

72725

25

It was the most FUN we've had together since . . .
um, yesterday.

Suddenly the porch light flicked on ☹!!

"OH, CRUD! Someone's coming outside!" I shouted.
"HIDE!!"

We quickly dove into some nearby bushes and then
cautiously peeked out.

The front door opened, and we saw a figure walk down the sidewalk.

"Hurry up and go potty already, Fifi! It's freezing out here!" said a very familiar voice.

It was MACKENZIE ☹!!

OH, CRUD! I'm going to have to finish writing this diary entry later. I'm trying to vent about some VERY personal and private stuff and my MOM just barged into my bedroom without even knocking!

She said that for Family Sharing Time, we're all going with Brianna to see the latest Princess Sugar Plum movie.

And then we're having dinner at Queasy Cheesy.

AGGGGHHHHHH! SPLAT!!

That was me BARFING!

I don't know which I HATE more, Princess Sugar Plum movies or Queasy Cheesy!

I guess I'm STILL traumatised by that time MacKenzie videotaped Brianna and me dancing at Queasy Cheesy and put it on YouTube.

Gotta STOP writing in my diary even though I don't want to!!

TO BE CONTINUED . . .

So, where was I before I was so RUDELY interrupted (tapping chin, trying to remember)?

Oh! Right in the middle of the Great Toilet Paper Caper!

"Hurry up and go potty already, Fifi! It's freezing out here!" MacKenzie complained to her poodle.

Although her humongous garden had more landscaping than a city park, that stupid dog decided to PIDDLE on EXACTLY the same BUSH we were hiding in.

OMG! We didn't move a muscle. We didn't even dare breathe!

"What's wrong, Fifi? There's nothing there but bushes. Let's go back inside now."

We breathed a collective sigh of relief. WHEW!

Then, without warning, Fifi darted under the bushes and lunged at us, barking like a rabid pit bull.

"Bark, bark, bark! Bark-bark! Bark! Bark-bark!"

"AAAAAAAAAHHH!" we screamed as we fell over each other trying to scramble out of the bushes.

Of course, we scared the juice out of MacKenzie. She gaped in horror and screamed even louder tha~ us. "AAAAAAAAAHHH!!"

Realising that MacKenzie had actually seen o~ faces, we just clung to each other and scr~ louder. "AAAAAAAAAHHH!!!"

Which freaked MacKenzie out even more and made her scream louder yet. "AAAAAAAAAAHHHH!!"

All of that barking, freaking and screaming in the bushes went on for what seemed like FOREVER.

"NIKKI?! CHLOE?! ZOEY?!" MacKenzie finally sputtered. "OMG! You guys nearly scared me to death! WHAT are you doing out here in the middle of the night?!"

"Um, would you believe we were taking a little walk and got lost in your bushes?" I asked.

"NO! I wouldn't!" she said, folding her arms and glaring at us.

"I didn't think so. . ." I muttered. "Well, it was nice chatting with you. But we really must be going—"

"Not so fast! YOU have some explaining to do. WHY are you snooping around my house? And WHY is the Easter Bunny here on New Year's Day?!"

~~The Easter Bunny~~ Chloe, Zoey and I just stared at the ground.

Hey, I may be a coward, but at least I'm an HONEST one. I felt morally obligated to te MacKenzie the truth.

"We . . . um . . . were sort of in the middle of toilet-papering y-your house," I stammered.

"You were WHAT?!" MacKenzie turned around and finally noticed the streamers of toilet paper dangling from her trees. "No way! Nikki, I can't believe you would actually—"

"It's NOT her fault. It was MY idea," Zoey said in my defence. "I dared her to do it."

"Yeah, but the Truth or Dare game was MY idea," Chloe said, hanging her head. "That makes ME totally responsible."

"Come on! Do you REALLY think I'm STUPID enough to actually believe you naive little dorks could pull off a majorly deviant prank like this?" MacKenzie sneered.

Our mouths dropped open in shock.

"Um . . . YES! We think you're STUPID! And NO! We're NOT so naive that we couldn't pull off a prank like this," I shot back.

33

"Yeah, right! You can't even LIE convincingly," MacKenzie scoffed.

Then she gave us the evil eye, like we were something her poodle had just left on the pavement.

MACKENZIE, GIVING US THE EVIL EYE

That's when it dawned on me that she didn't believe a single word we were saying. I was . . . FLABBERGASTED!

"Obviously, some really cute guys did this to get

my attention! Boys are SO obsessed with me."

MacKenzie giggled and batted her eyes like she was flirting with some invisible crush only she could see.

"Hmmm . . . I bet it was Brady and some of the football jocks. Or maybe Theodore and his nerdy band members. . ."

Then she put her hands over her heart and swooned.

"OMG! I think I know who did it! BRANDON!!" she squealed. "Nikki, you must be SO jealous that he toilet-papered MY house and not YOURS! Eat your heart out, hon!"

"MacKenzie, I have seven words for you. YouNeedToGetAClue.com!" I said, staring right into her beady little eyes. "But since we made this mess in your garden, I guess it's only fair that we clean it up."

Suddenly she narrowed her eyes at me.

"You came over here in the middle of the night to clean up the toilet paper in MY garden?! But WHY? I bet you didn't want me to see it. Then I would never know that Brandon is CRUSHING on me! Is that it?"

I rolled my eyes at her. "No, MacKenzie! Brandon had nothing to do with—"

"You're LYING! It's MY toilet paper! So don't even think about touching it! If Brandon went to all this trouble, he must REALLY like me. And that's why you're hanging around here trying to UNDERMINE my love life!"

ME?!! Undermine HER love life??!!

SORRY! But I'm WAY too busy undermining my OWN love life. Which is why I don't have one.

MacKenzie thinks the whole world revolves around her, and I wanted to burst her little bubble SO badly. But talking to a SNOBBY AIRHEAD like her is a lot like eating a can of SARDINES . . .

POINTLESS and NAUSEATING!

← MACKENZIE

SARDINES →

"Whatever, MacKenzie!" I sighed. "Believe what you want. We toilet-papered your house! We're TIRED!! And we're going HOME!!"

Chloe, Zoey and I picked up the empty cardboard toilet paper rolls strewn across the garden and headed towards the pavement.

Hey, we were vandals, but we WEREN'T litterbugs!

"PUT THOSE BACK! THEY'RE MINE!" MacKenzie

screeched. "Or I'll call the cops! It's illegal to take stuff from private property. LOSERS!"

Chloe, Zoey and I froze and looked at each other in disbelief. Then we tossed the cardboard toilet paper rolls BACK into her garden.

It was pure INSANITY!

"Oh! And by the way . . . HAPPY NEW YEAR!!" MacKenzie chirped, all happy and friendlylike.

Did I mention that girl is SCHIZOID?

We walked back to Zoey's house in complete silence. The entire experience was just . . . SURREAL!

Suddenly Chloe started to snicker. Then Zoey caught the giggles. Finally I did too. We were laughing so hard we were practically staggering down the pavement.

"Thank goodness MacKenzie didn't believe us.

Otherwise, she'd probably be burying our dead bodies in her back garden," I chuckled.

"Hey! We tried to tell her the truth. But her ego is so huge it has stretch marks." Zoey snorted.

In spite of everything, I think my BFFs and I learned two very valuable life lessons that night.

1. Revenge is NOT the answer and

2. No one can make a complete FOOL out of MacKenzie better than . . . MACKENZIE!

The Great Toilet Paper Caper was an epic FAIL!

But, personally, I'm just happy we made it out of there alive.

It looks like my new year is off to a really good start!

☺!!

SATURDAY, JANUARY 4

Guess what I got in the mail today?!

An invitation to . . .

BRANDON'S BIRTHDAY PARTY!!

SQUEEEEEEE ☺!!

I was so happy I did my Snoopy "happy dance".

Brandon's birthday party is on Friday, January 31, and I can hardly wait!

Chloe, Zoey and I are invited, but MacKenzie isn't. I have to admit, I feel a little sorry for her ☹.

NOT!! Too bad, MacKenzie ☺!

She was SO SUPERjealous about Brandon's party that she actually tried to HYPNOTIZE him into giving her an invitation by smiling, batting her eyes and twirling her hair. But it didn't work.

Anyway, I don't have the slightest idea what I'm going to get Brandon for his birthday. But at least I have enough money saved up to get him something nice.

I was thinking about taking him out to dinner at a quaint little Italian restaurant. And we could share a romantic plate of spaghetti like in my favourite Disney movie, *Lady and the Tramp*. SQUEEE!

Speaking of restaurants, Brianna and I went to this brand-new place in the mall called Crazy Burger. They make these HUGE gourmet burgers that are supposed to be delicious.

However, after placing my order, I wasn't so sure the food was all that healthy . . .

43

I wanted to say, Um . . . NEVER MIND!

But I was absolutely STARVING!

I was SO hungry I could have eaten that foam-rubber burger right off the top of his ridiculously tacky hat.

Plastic googly eyes and all.

And get this. Those ridiculous hats were for sale for $7.99. But WHO in their right mind would even buy one of those things?!

Anyway, that burger was superyummy and juicy. Brianna loved hers too.

Hey! Maybe Brandon and I could have a fancy, candlelight dinner at Crazy Burger for his birthday!

NOT!

☺!!

SUNDAY, JANUARY 5

Today I received some exciting news from Trevor Chase, the producer of the hit television show _15 Minutes of Fame_ and the judge of the Westchester Country Day Talent Showcase.

Back in November, I put together a band called Actually, I'm Not Really Sure Yet. And yes! I know it's the craziest band name ever. We were supposed to be called Dorkalicious. But MacKenzie stuck her big nose in my personal business and pretty much messed up everything.

Her dance group won the WCD Talent Showcase and a chance to audition for the TV show.

But Trevor was so impressed with MY band that he asked us to record an original song that we'd written called "Dorks Rule!"

Can you believe THAT?

Anyway, I was just hanging out in my bedroom

writing in my diary when I finally got the follow-up call that he'd promised . . .

OMG! YES, MR CHASE, WE'D LOVE TO MEET WITH YOU ON SATURDAY, FEBRUARY 8!

I called Chloe, Zoey, Brandon, Violet and Theo and gave them the fantastic news! We decided our band would start practising again the week before Mr Chase was scheduled to arrive.

OMG! Wouldn't it be great if we went on tour and opened for Lady Gaga or One Direction?! We could take this music thing and run with it.

Just imagine what our lives would be like if we became pop stars. We'd be on the covers of all the teen magazines and maybe even have our own really cute-smelling perfume.

The best part is that Brandon and I could star in a blockbuster movie called *Middle School Musical*. About two dorks in LOVE! SQUEEEEE!!

I smell an Academy Award for Best Movie!

Hey, it could happen. Eat your heart out, MacKenzie!

☺!!

Today was the first day of school after our two-week winter break.

I have to admit, I was NOT looking forward to seeing MacKenzie.

I guess I was just SUPERworried about Chloe, Zoey and me getting in trouble for toilet-papering her house.

Would our parents be called to the school?

Would we get detention?

Would we be suspended?

Would we be arrested?

However, I would have gladly chosen ANY of these horrible outcomes over listening to MacKenzie BLAB on and on and on about her nonexistent SECRET ADMIRER. . . !!!

NIKKI! I DON'T KNOW WHAT YOU LITTLE TROLLS WERE DOING AT MY HOUSE THAT NIGHT. BUT I'M WARNING YOU, KEEP YOUR NOSE OUT OF MY PERSONAL BUSINESS!

That girl was all up in my face like bad breath.

"MacKenzie, I already apologised and offered to clean up everything. But as I explained before, Chloe, Zoey and I were just goofing around."

"You liar! You're just jealous because Brandon is my secret admirer! Sorry, but he likes ME and not YOU! It's not MY fault your face looks like it caught on fire and someone tried to put it out with a fork!"

"Well, it's not MY fault you're such an AIRHEAD that if you open your mouth I can hear the ocean!" I shot back.

"I'm warning you, Maxwell. Just back off!! Or you'll be sorry. You don't belong at this school anyway."

When MacKenzie said those words, a cold chill ran down my spine. But she was absolutely right!

I DIDN'T belong at her school. Unfortunately, I was attending on a bug extermination scholarship that my dad had arranged.

MacKenzie is the ONLY student who knows my embarrassing secret. And if the other students find out, I am going to just . . . crawl into . . . my locker and . . . DIE!

MacKenzie gave me a big smile as she hurled one final insult.

"Oh, by the way, I LOVE what you did with your hair today. How did you get it to come out of one nostril like that?"

Then she slammed her locker shut and sashayed away. I just HATE it when MacKenzie sashays.

By lunchtime the whole school was gossiping that Brandon was crushing on MacKenzie.

The story was that he had spent an entire hour toilet-papering her house as a practical joke to get her attention. Then he'd left a dozen roses and a box of Godiva chocolates at her front door, rung her doorbell and run away. Nikki Maxwell was SO jealous that she had showed up in the middle of the night with her BFFs to try and take down the toilet paper so she could ruin MacKenzie's surprise.

OMG! That entire story was SO ridiculous, I was pretty sure no one would believe it. Besides, MacKenzie had no proof WHATSOEVER . . .

Except her framed photograph of it all!

She was so proud, she'd actually taken a picture of her house with her mobile. I heard she had even posted it online!

And during lunch, all the CCP girls were crowded around and swooning over her photo like it was a baby picture of Justin Bieber or somebody.

But I was more worried about Brandon than anyone. He had enough stuff going on in his life without MacKenzie and me creating additional drama.

I just hope all of this idle gossip won't damage our friendship.

Although, I have a really bad feeling that damaging our friendship is EXACTLY what MacKenzie is trying to do.

☹!!

AAAAAAAAAAAHH!

(That was me screaming!)

Right now I'm having a complete meltdown!

WHY?

Because when I went to breakfast this morning, I saw a strange man in a fancy business suit standing in our kitchen.

And get this!

My mom handed him a cup of coffee and then gave him a big, fat kiss.

Right on the lips!

I was about to scream, "MOM! WHAT ARE YOU DOING?! YOU'RE MARRIED TO DAD!!"

But then I realised the man WAS my dad!

I have to admit, he cleans up really nicely.

"Dad, you look great! What's the occasion?" I asked as I took a huge bite of my strawberry Pop-Tart.

"Well, dear, due to Maxwell's Bug Extermination's great reputation, I just might have an exciting new business opportunity." Dad beamed proudly.

Hey, I didn't want to rain on his parade, but the guy rides around town with a two-metre tall plastic bug on top of his van.

I mean, just how GOOD could his rep actually be?!

I'm just sayin'!

He continued, "I have a meeting this morning with the owner of the most successful property management company in the city, Hollister Holdings, Inc."

At first I just stared at my dad with my eyes practically bulging out of my head.

Then I choked and sputtered . . .

OMG! DAD! DITH YOU JUTH THAY "HOLLITHER"?!

It felt like a huge chunk of pastry had got stuck inside my throat. Or maybe pure dread and a massively severe anxiety attack were stopping me breathing.

"Yep! I'll be meeting with Marshall Hollister. Your mom says his daughter goes to your school and she's a really good friend of yours."

Suddenly I felt really light-headed, and the room started to spin!

"But, Dad! How do you know it's a business meeting? Maybe he wants to talk to you about something else, like . . . um, I don't know! Something kind of surprising or shocking, that could involve lots of, you know, um . . . toilet paper . . . and trees. . ."

"HUH?!" Dad looked at me, totally perplexed. "I don't even KNOW this guy. What ELSE would Moneybags Marshall want to talk to me about but a business deal?"

"I—I don't have the slightest idea!" I stammered.

That's when I looked deep into my father's eyes and desperately pleaded with him:

"DAD! PLEASE! DON'T GO TO THAT MEETING!

I HAVE A REALLY BAD FEELING ABOUT IT!
IF YOU REALLY LOVE ME, YOU WON'T GO!
PLEASE, PROMISE ME!"

But he must have thought I was just joking around or something, because he chuckled and kissed my forehead.

"Boy! You and your mother are more nervous about this meeting than I am. But don't worry, I'm a shrewd and savage shark when it comes to business. I'm TOTALLY in control. Just call me MR BIZ!"

"Well, Mr Biz!" My mom giggled. "Your tie is floating in your coffee and you have jam in your moustache. I think a shrewd and savage shark needs to run upstairs to wash his face and change his tie!"

Dad fished his tie out of his coffee and stared at it in total disgust.

"Aww, shucks! This is my really pretty POWER tie! Now it's RUINED!" he whined like a five-year-old.

MY DAD, THE SHREWD AND SAVAGE BUSINESS SHARK

It was quite obvious! MacKenzie had finally ratted on me, and now HER dad wanted to talk to MY dad.

Which means at some point in the immediate future, my parents are going to KILL ME!!

I was torn as to whether I should pack my suitcase and sneak away to become a teenage bag-lady BEFORE or AFTER school.

But the least I could do was try to warn my BFFs, Chloe and Zoey, that MacKenzie's dad was probably going to be contacting THEIR parents next.

So it's settled.

I'll run away AFTER school.

☹!!

WEDNESDAY, JANUARY 8

WHAT in the world is going on around here?!

MacKenzie has been superNICE to me for the past two days!

And even though HER dad had that meeting with MY dad yesterday, she's STILL bragging to everyone that Brandon toilet-papered her house.

Which makes no sense WHATSOEVER!

And weirder yet, my dad and mom haven't uttered a single word about me being . . .

1. in REALLY BIG TROUBLE,

2. a MAJOR DISAPPOINTMENT to them, or

3. a POOR ROLE MODEL FOR MY YOUNGER SISTER, BRIANNA

. . . and it's driving me completely NUTS!

I started thinking they were using some kind of Dr Phil-inspired "parental reverse psychology" thing on me as punishment. Just to watch me squirm.

Because, I swear, I'm feeling so NERVOUS and so GUILTY right now I'm ready to confess what I did, give myself a stern lecture, take away all of my own privileges and then ground MYSELF for the rest of the year.

But as soon as I got home from school today, it all started to make sense.

My dad was out in the front garden with all of this fancy new high-tech extermination equipment.

OMG! He had an X-14 Bug-B-Gone Power Sprayer with twenty-four assorted EZ Snap-on Nozzle Tips, a BreatheMore Ventilated Face Mask, a PowerPack UltraLight Double Canister Backpack and a poly-cotton-blend blue designer uniform by Tommy Hilfiger.

Dad had filled the sprayer with water and was

playing with it like a little boy trying out a new Super Soaker water gun or something.

However, the thing that totally freaked me out was NOT the shiny new blue van parked nearby, but the company NAME plastered across it. . . .

That's when I realised my dad had pretty much sold his soul to the devil!

As far as I was concerned, the Maxwell family was now OWNED by the Hollister family.

Dad waved at me and smiled. "Hi, honey! How was school today?"

"Horrible! Dad, where did you get all of this new stuff?"

"Oh, it's not mine. Yet, anyway. That meeting with Marshall Hollister yesterday went really well. He owns seven apartment complexes and four office buildings and plans to expand this year. His pest-control technician just retired and he wants me to stand in for a few weeks until he finds a new guy and trains—"

"So it's just temporary?!" I interrupted. "Thank goodness!" I could feel a weight lifting off my shoulders.

"Marshall said he's heard good things about my

65

extermination work at your school from his daughter. And he says she HATES everyone. Even him!" Dad chuckled.

"But what about YOUR customers? How are you going to have time to run your own business AND work for Mr Hollister?"

"Actually, he said I could set my own hours. And I get to use his new van and all of his fancy equipment. But the best part is the extra income. Working for Mr Hollister is a fantastic opportunity, and I plan to take full advantage of it."

That's when I had the most horrible thought!

What if my dad quits his job to work full-time for Mr Hollister?!! Then I'd lose my scholarship at WCD and have to transfer to a new school!!

Maybe that was MacKenzie's master plan?!! I felt my heart drop into my boots.

I could NOT believe my dad was ruining my life like

this! But I knew this was NOT really about him.

It was about that big blowout I'd had with MacKenzie on New Year's Eve.

And now Dad's fairy godfather, Moneybags Marshall Hollister, had appeared out of thin air and offered to turn him into a bug-zapping Cinderella.

DAD'S FAIRY GODFATHER

OMG!

DAD →

67

It was MACKENZIE who was ruining my life!! As USUAL!

"Don't worry, dear. I'm completely in control. Just call me—"

I finished his sentence. "Mr Biz! The shrewd and savage business shark, right?"

"Right!" Dad said, giving me a big hug. Then he went back to spraying water on his pretend snow bugs or something.

And I went straight to my bedroom and cried for an entire hour.

Now I'm sitting on the edge of my bed sulking. Which for some reason always makes me feel a lot better.

I'm just totally bummed about the possibility that I might have to leave my friends at WCD.

WHY is my life just one deep . . . dreary . . . cesspool of . . . heartbreak and . . . disappointment?!

ME, GAZING INTO THE CESSPOOL
THAT IS MY LIFE!

Judging by how much my dad is loving his new job, I'll probably be transferring for SURE!

I guess my only option is to try and hold on to my bug extermination scholarship for as long as possible.

Which is going to be next to impossible with MacKenzie out to destroy my life.

AAAAAAAAAAAAAAH!!

That was me screaming in frustration!

I'm supposed to be in my first class right now.
But instead, I'm hiding out in the girls' toilets,
writing in my diary, and trying NOT to have a
nervous breakdown.

I just had a big fight with MacKenzie, and now this
whole Great Toilet Paper Caper thing has turned
into a major FIASCO!!

It all started when I stopped by the office to
get a copy of our WCD student handbook. I was
SUPERworried and was dying to find out what the
school policy was on pranks.

And guess who was the student office assistant?

JESSICA ☺!! Who, BTW, is MacKenzie Hollister's
FF. Jessica is supposed to work in there only

ONE hour a day during her study hall.

But I'm starting to suspect she SECRETLY lives in
the school office or something. . .

I just knew Jessica was going to blab all of my personal business to MacKenzie.

But she didn't have to, because the very last person I wanted to see was sitting right there with Jessica, gossiping and doing her nails . . .

MACKENZIE ☹!!

Maybe I'm just paranoid, but it seems like those two girls are forever popping up in my life at exactly the WRONG time!

Like some kind of living, breathing, talking, gloss-addicted, um . . . PIMPLES!

I wanted to turn right around and run out of that place screaming. But instead, I cleared my throat, smiled and said really friendlylike, "Um, sorry to interrupt you guys. But I'd like a copy of the student handbook, please."

Jessica looked up from polishing her nails and just glared at me like I was something that had just crawled out of the sewer. I could tell she was SUPERannoyed when she said . . .

NIKKI, CAN'T YOU SEE I'M BUSY? MY NAILS WON'T BE DRY FOR AT LEAST ANOTHER TWELVE MINUTES! COME BACK NEXT WEEK.

JESSICA, →
DOING HER
NAILS

I could not believe Jessica actually said that right to my face. She's, like, the WORST office assistant EVER!

That's when MacKenzie glared at me all evil-like. Then she grabbed a handbook from the back counter and very rudely tossed it right at me . . .

"Actually, Jessica, Nikki really needs a handbook right now so she can read the part about how student pranks and destroying personal property are an automatic suspension from school. It's on page one twenty-eight. Read it and weep, Nikki!"

My hands were shaking so badly, I could barely hold the book. I turned to page 128 and quickly read the page.

"Wait a minute!" I said. "It says right here, 'Student pranking and practical jokes are discouraged and punishable by after-school detention. Purposely

75

destroying property may result in a suspension from school.' No one destroyed any property, MacKenzie."

"Well, I think you DESERVE to be kicked out of school! Putting toilet paper in trees is not so bad. But EGGING a house can damage property. And I thought I saw eggs all over the place that night. Didn't you see them? Those eggs probably damaged my property."

"OMG, MacKenzie! You know good and well there WEREN'T any EGGS. And WE didn't throw any. . . !"

"Well, SOMEBODY did! And if it wasn't you guys, maybe it was . . . I don't know . . . my secret admirer. . . ?!" she said as an evil grin spread across her face.

"I can't believe you're actually accusing Brandon of toilet-papering your house AND throwing EGGS?!! How can you just LIE like that?! Especially knowing he could be suspended from school!" I screamed at that girl.

MacKenzie stared at me with her beady little eyes for what seemed like FOREVER.

"Actually, Nikki, I'm sure I could totally forget about the whole egg thing if someone was able to get me and Jessica invitations to Brandon's party. . ."

Then she batted her eyes at me all innocentlike.

I was so shocked I almost fell over.

I could NOT believe my ears!

I had to restrain myself from reaching over and SLAPPING that girl SILLY.

I would never, ever egg anyone or anything because it's wrong.

But right then I was so MAD at MacKenzie for being such a deceitful, manipulative, pathological LIAR that I couldn't help but imagine what I'd love to do with a dozen eggs. . .

"Okay, MacKenzie. And what if someone DOESN'T come up with invites. . . ?" I asked.

"Oh, I don't know. Maybe I'll just write about the entire event in my little gossip column — er, I mean Fashion and Current Events column for the school newspaper. Once Principal Winston finds out, SOMEONE is going to be suspended! That's for sure. So it's YOUR choice."

Hey, you do the crime, you do the time. Toilet-papering MacKenzie's house was wrong, and I don't mind doing after-school detention for it. I totally deserve that.

But no one threw eggs or destroyed her property.

And MacKenzie making up malicious LIES to get us suspended unless we cough up party invites is just WRONG on so many levels!

Losing my WCD scholarship because my dad decides to work full-time for MacKenzie's dad is really BAD! But the possibility of Brandon getting kicked out of school because of MY stupid prank would be horrendously UNFAIR!

There's just no way I can let this happen.

There has to be SOMETHING I can do to stop MacKenzie?!!

AAAAAAAAAAAAAAAHHH!

That was me screaming in frustration.

AGAIN! ☹!!

FRIDAY, JANUARY 10

I barely got any sleep last night.

I just lay there, wide awake, trying to figure out how to stop MacKenzie.

I realise I could simply ~~ask~~ BEG Brandon to invite MacKenzie and Jessica to his party.

But then it would be MY fault if those snobby

little drama queens RUINED his birthday.

I wouldn't blame Brandon for wondering whether I was a true friend of his or just a mindless little puppet for MacKenzie.

So, my ONLY option is to try and get a position on the school newspaper.

That way, I can at least try to stop her from printing stuff in her gossip column about Brandon, Chloe, Zoey and me that could get us kicked out of school.

If I keep a really close eye on MacKenzie, I can shut her down BEFORE she makes any trouble, by reporting her to the newspaper adviser.

The BAD news is that I know nothing whatsoever about writing for a school newspaper. Except for maybe THREE things:

1. It has writing, and I'm seriously addicted to writing in my diary.

2. It has comic strips and cartoons, and I'm seriously addicted to drawing.

3. It has my crush, Brandon, ~~and I'm seriously addicted to him~~.

However, the GOOD news is that there's a meeting next week for students interested in joining the newspaper staff.

I'm just praying all of this works!

During gym I casually mentioned my plan to Chloe and Zoey, and they thought it was a wonderful idea.

Of course, I purposely left out the part about me needing to join the newspaper because MacKenzie was ruthlessly plotting to get all of us kicked out of school by spreading lies and untruths!

And when I explained to them that I was really worried because the only serious writing I'd ever done was in my diary, Chloe and Zoey assured me that I'd do just fine.

They said only an insanely untalented person could obsessively write in a diary like I did and STILL be a superCRUDDY writer.

It was SO SWEET of them to compliment me like that.

I think.

I got really emotional and my eyes started to tear up a little during our deep knee bends. . .

ME, GETTING SUPEREMOTIONAL DURING OUR DEEP KNEE BENDS

And get this!!

Chloe and Zoey said they would help with my newspaper projects.

I can ALWAYS count on them to be there for me.
I'm SO lucky to have BFFs like Chloe and Zoey!

They also mentioned how joining the school
newspaper would be the perfect opportunity
for Brandon and me to spend more quality time
together.

OMG! I hadn't really thought about THAT ☺!!!

I bet MacKenzie is going to be SO jealous!

And it was Chloe and Zoey's brilliant idea for me
to ask Brandon to help me find a position, since he's
SUPERfamiliar with the newspaper and the way it
works.

He's going to be shocked and surprised when I
pop up at the newspaper office during lunch on
Monday.

We haven't really talked much this week because he's
been unusually quiet.

I'm sure he's heard all of the ridiculous gossip about him toilet-papering MacKenzie's house and leaving her lavish gifts because he's crushing on her.

But the CRUELEST thing about all of this is that MacKenzie is actually setting Brandon up to take the blame for something I did, unless I compromise our friendship and arrange for her to get invited to his party.

I really want to set the record straight and tell everyone what REALLY happened that night.

But the last thing I need right now is to get into World War III with MacKenzie. Especially when the casualties could end up being people I really care about.

Like Chloe and Zoey.

And Brandon too.

And OMG! I almost forgot. Even my DAD!

MACKENZIE AND I
DECLARE WAR ON
EACH OTHER!

Anyway, I can't imagine Brandon and me working together on the newspaper.

EVERY. SINGLE. DAY!

SQUEEEE!! Who would have thunk such an awful situation could turn out so . . . GOOD?!

☺!!

For once, I'm actually looking forward to going to school on Monday.

I can't wait to tell Brandon my plans.

And once I join the newspaper staff, I'll be able to watch MacKenzie like a hawk so she can't stir up trouble.

The only thing that STILL worries me is my writing skills. Because I AM joining a NEWSPAPER.

I mean, this could be as disastrous as signing up for an ice-skating charity event when you don't even know how to ice-skate. DUH!

I remember the time I had to write my secret family recipe for Crispy Squares in our class recipe book back in primary school. The recipe book was a Mother's Day present.

My grandma said that recipe had been in my family

for sixteen generations. Apparently my ancestor, who was a Pilgrim, served it as the official dessert at the very first Thanksgiving feast back in 1621.

So I was more than a little SURPRISED when, a couple of months ago, I was reading the back of a cereal box and found the EXACT SAME RECIPE!!

ME, READING OUR SECRET FAMILY RECIPE ON THE CEREAL BOX

Can you believe that?!

OMG!

Especially after all of that stuff my grandma had said about it being in our family since 1621.

I was SHOCKED and APPALLED that people could actually be so blatantly DISHONEST!

Whatever happened to honesty and integrity?!

I mean, that huge cereal company should be ASHAMED of themselves for STEALING our secret family recipe for Crispy Squares and plastering it all over their cereal boxes like that.

I personally think we should consider taking legal action or something.

However, since my writing skills weren't that good, the secret family recipe I wrote back in second grade was actually a little A LOT different from the one on the cereal box. . . .

~~Nikki~~ Nikki's Crispy Squares

(Secret Family Recipe)

~~ingridintz~~ Ingredients

1. 4 cups Crispy rice Bits cereal
2. One stick Butter
3. Something else (but I forgot what it was) ☹!

Directions

Place all ingredients in a pan
Cook over low heat.
Cool and eat.

ENJOY! ☺

THE FAMILY RECIPE I WROTE BACK IN
PRIMARY SCHOOL

It was actually kind of embarrassing because I accidentally left out one of the main ingredients from the recipe.

Hey, I was ONLY seven years old!

Although, if it's supposed to be a SECRET recipe, WHY would you BLAB all of the ingredients?

Anyway, my yummy butter-fried Crispy Squares had a lot LESS calories than the ones slathered with those sugary-sweet melted marshmallows.

Hmmm, now that I think about it . . .

Maybe my first article for the WCD school newspaper could be my delicious secret family recipe for Crispy Squares.

NOT!!

☺!!

SUNDAY, JANUARY 12

I can't believe it snowed another eight centimetres today!

I'm just so sick of this snow, and it's only January. I don't know if I can survive two more long, dreary, cold months of winter.

For spring break, MacKenzie and most of the CCPs will be going on holiday somewhere that's warm, sunny and exciting.

But not me! I'll probably be stuck at home helping my mom with SPRING CLEANING ☹!!

I'd give anything to be relaxing on a sunny, warm beach in Hawaii right now. How cool would THAT be?!

So when Mom insisted that I take Brianna outside to let her play in the snow, I grabbed some sunglasses and beach toys and decided to make lemonade out of lemons! Right in our garden . . .

Suddenly the weather felt so tropical, I almost got a sunburn just standing there admiring our work.

All Brianna and I needed were our swimsuits and a beach towel, and we could have joined in on the fun in the sun, surf and snow.

Am I not BRILLIANT?!

☺!!

Today is the big day! I plan to drop in on Brandon and ask him for help with joining the newspaper staff.

I wore a really cute outfit that my grandma bought me during her last visit. Chloe and Zoey said I looked really smart and professional.

I think they were right, because while I was at my locker putting on lip gloss, MacKenzie stopped by to get lunch money and eyeballed me all evil-like.

I knew she was dying to ask me why I was so dressed up. But I just ignored her.

I definitely wouldn't be surprised if she actually tried to spy on me.

Hey, the little weasel has done it before!

I decided to channel my inner "smart reporter" so I would feel more confident.

97

A pencil behind the ear for emergency notes and flair? Check.

Shimmery Savvy Girl lip gloss? Check.

Spearmint-fresh breath for interviews? Check.

Notepad for capturing my brilliant thoughts (and awesome doodles)? Check.

Intellectual-looking and slightly uncomfortable pumps? Check.

I was trying my hardest to be a sassy, journalistic girl genius and NOT the slightly illiterate writer I felt like inside.

Finally, I took a deep breath and headed down the hall and into the newspaper office.

I scanned the room for Brandon, and as usual, I recognised his shaggy hair behind one of the computer monitors.

OMG! I suddenly felt very queasy and light-headed. But in a really GOOD way ☺!!

Mostly I was worried that throwing up the strawberry-banana smoothie I had chugged at my locker for lunch would undermine my "smart reporter" image.

"Nikki!" Brandon smiled, waved, and gestured for me to come over. "What's up?"

"Actually, I just decided to sign up for the newspaper. And since the new members meeting is after school today, I thought maybe you could help me find a position and give me some tips. Since you're a SUPERtalented photojournalist and stuff," I said, blushing profusely.

Brandon blinked in surprise. "No way! You're kidding! Right?"

"Hey! I've got a pad of paper and a pen, and I'm NOT afraid to use 'em!" I teased.

BRANDON AND I DISCUSS ME JOINING THE SCHOOL NEWSPAPER!

"Very cool! I'd be happy to help you out, Nikki. I can't wait to read your first article."

"Um . . . thanks!" I plastered a big smile across my face, but inside I was a nervous wreck.

Sure, I'm a scribbling whiz kid when it comes to my diary. But writing boring, serious, newsworthy-type stuff, NOT so much.

I needed to pull off a major miracle or the only thing Brandon was going to get out of any article I wrote was a really good . . . NAP.

Brandon quickly pulled up on his computer a list of the open positions and started reading them aloud.

"Well, let's see. There're six open positions right now. Assistant fashion editor, sports, news . . . Hey, look at this! We need a photo layout artist. YOU'D be perfect for that!"

"OMG!" I squealed. "That means we could spend a lot of time together! Er, I mean, time t-together . . .

you know, w—working on those photo layout, um, thingies. . ." I stammered.

"Now, THAT would be way cool!" Brandon brushed his bangs out of his eyes and gave me a crooked smile.

I just HATED when he did that to me. I had a massive Roller-Coaster Syndrome attack right there in front of him. It was SO embarrassing!

I lost total control and actually screamed,

"WHEEEEEEEEEEEEE!"

But I just said it inside my head so no one else heard it but me.

That's when he kind of stared at me and I stared back at him. Then we both smiled.

And after that I couldn't help but stare at him, and of course he stared back at me. Then we both blushed.

All of this staring, smiling and blushing seemed to go on, like, FOREVER!

BRANDON AND ME, STARING, SMILING
AND BLUSHING

Brandon and I spent the rest of the lunch hour just hanging out and talking.

He even showed me some of his photos he planned to enter into a national competition next month.

And get this! We actually walked to bio together!

I can't wait to tell Chloe and Zoey how well everything went.

Although working on the newspaper is going to be fun, I have to remember to stay focused on the real task.

Shutting down MacKenzie!

Hey! That girl started this war, but I'M going to FINISH it!

I'M THE CHAMP!!

Right now I'm SO frustrated I could just . . .

SCREAM!!

But all I can do is sit here in my geometry class totally lost (as usual), pretending that:

1. I care about irregular quadrilaterals and

2. my life is NOT the vapid waste dump that it IS.

About seven new people showed up for the newspaper meeting. A half dozen staff members came to answer questions and serve as mentors, including Brandon and MacKenzie.

I really liked our journalism intern. Mainly because she was actually SANE (unlike our adviser). She started the meeting by saying, "Hi, everyone. I'd like to welcome our new members and thank you for coming today. My name is Lauren Walsh. I'm a senior at Westchester Country Day High School and a journalism intern. Mr Zimmerman, our adviser, will be here in a few minutes. He requested that I have all the new people sit in the front, so let's do that right now."

MacKenzie huffed and rolled her eyes at the prospect of having to give up her seat to a newbie. "This is SO lame! I'm NOT moving."

That girl is SUCH a drama queen. I was like, "Come on, MacKenzie. Just lose the attitude. Are you THAT attached to your desk? You're acting like you're about to put up matching curtains or something!"

But I just said that inside my head so no one else heard it but me.

Soon a middle-aged man in jeans and a wrinkled blazer shuffled in.

He carried an empty jumbo-size coffee cup, and he had a messenger bag over his shoulder that was so full he left a trail of papers on the floor.

MR ZIMMERMAN

His hair was messy, and the stubble on his face was so long it was about to grow into a hippie beard.

107

He took a seat at his cluttered desk and just stared at us in disgust.

It was like we were something unpleasant he wanted to scrape off the bottom of his shoe.

Then he popped a few sweets into his mouth from the Scooby-Doo PEZ dispenser sitting on his desk.

After munching loudly on the sweets for what seemed like forever, he finally spoke, his eyes still glued on the kids in the front row.

"Lauren, WHO are these people?!"

"These are the students interested in joining the newspaper, Mr Zimmerman."

"And why are they sitting there staring at me?"

"Actually, they're seated in the front row, just like you requested," Lauren answered.

"Very interesting," he said drily. "Let me ask you something, boys and girls."

He got up and paced the floor.

"How many of you have NEVER worked for a newspaper before?"

Everyone in the newbie row excitedly raised their hand, including me.

"Okay. Then none of you have experience," he said, lowering his voice to barely a whisper.

The room was so quiet you could hear a pin drop.

"Well, today is your lucky day because I'm going to let you in on a little secret. You're about to experience firsthand how the real world of journalism operates."

We all leaned forward in our seats, straining to hear the pearls of wisdom Zimmerman was about to bestow upon us.

"Listen carefully, boys and girls, because I'm only going to say this once. . ."

YOU'RE FIRED!

Okay! There was no question about it.

Zimmerman was totally INSANE!

The room broke into a panic.

The girl with braces sitting next to me started to cry.

Lauren looked startled.

"Um, sir. . ." She ran to him and whispered something in his ear.

"What do you mean, 'They're only kids'?" Mr Zimmerman snarked.

I couldn't hear what Lauren was saying, but I could tell he didn't like it.

"I can't? Really?"

Lauren shook her head.

"I see." Mr Zimmerman sighed. "I'll need another coffee to get through this."

Lauren scribbled his order in her notebook and rushed out the door.

"Make it black," he called after her. "My wife says I need to cut back on sugar."

Zimmerman popped another PEZ candy and continued pacing.

"Listen up, kids. We have six openings," he said, handing a sign-up sheet to the guy at the end of the row. "I expect you to eat, drink and breathe journalism from this day forward, or you won't survive in this business. MY reputation is on the line here. And I DON'T want it tarnished! Am I making myself clear?!"

Although it was a yes-or-no question, all of us just stared at him blankly.

We weren't that afraid of working for the newspaper.

But we were TERRIFIED of this unshaven LUNATIC rambling about "survival".

When I got the sign-up sheet, I held my breath and peeked at it. I was the fourth person to sign it, and the photo layout artist position was STILL available.

I quickly scribbled in my name next to it.

I had to restrain myself from breaking into my Snoopy "happy dance."

I passed the sheet to the girl with the braces.

"I could tell you some stories about my days with the *Wall Street Journal*," Mr Zimmerman continued. "But I won't. My wife says I need to let that go . . . and so does my therapist. Now, where is that sign-up sheet?" he asked, looking around the room nervously.

"Right here, Mr Zimmerman," MacKenzie said, waving the page in the air. "I have it."

She sashayed to the front of the room and handed it to him.

"Thank you, Miss Hollister. Both your dedication and teamwork are duly noted!"

It was like MacKenzie had totally brainwashed the guy or something.

She smiled and sashayed back to her seat.

I just HATE it when MacKenzie sashays.

Zimmerman quickly read over the list of names.

"Hmm, I see one of you changed your mind about making this serious commitment. Good! I'd much rather you quit now than waste my time."

I tried not to stare at the girl with the braces. She looked like she was about to burst into tears again.

"I have very high expectations for all of you. And just remember, it's a jungle out there!"

Zimmerman called up the newbies one by one and introduced them to the newspaper staff person they would be working with.

I waited anxiously for him to call my name.

I was a little confused when Marcy, the girl with the braces, was assigned to work with MacKenzie as an assistant editor for fashion.

Since she'd been in tears for most of the meeting, I had assumed she was the person who had quit.

"Hi, I'm Marcy, and I just moved here last semester from Boise, Idaho! I can't believe I'm actually going to be working with you, MacKenzie!" Marcy gushed.

"And I can't believe I'm actually going to be working with YOU!" MacKenzie said, scrunching up her nose like she smelled a funky foot odour.

"I'm NOT a fashionista. But I did design and sew an entire wardrobe for my Barbie doll collection." Marcy beamed proudly.

"How quaint! For our first assignment, we're going to tackle an emergency makeover. Fab-N-Flirty Fashions is having a big sale," MacKenzie said as she scribbled madly on her notepad. "Let's meet at the mall immediately after school today."

"OMG! That sounds so exciting! WHO'S getting the makeover?" Marcy asked.

I felt really sorry for that poor girl.

Marcy hadn't quit just yet. But since she was stuck with MacKenzie, it was only a matter of time.

I gave her twenty-four hours. Or less.

I turned my attention back to Mr Zimmerman.

"And last but not least, we're going to pair the photo layout artist position with . . . let's see . . ."

Brandon! Brandon! Brandon! I screamed silently.

"Okay, how about . . . BRANDON."

YES!! I turned around and flashed Brandon a big smile. I could not believe we were actually going to be working together.

"Brandon, you'll be mentoring our new photo layout artist. . ."

ME! I whispered dreamily to myself.

". . . BRITNEY CHUNG," Zimmerman announced.

I felt like I had just been punched in the stomach.

Britney, a CCP girl, scrambled out of her seat and immediately started making goo-goo eyes at Brandon.

There had to be some kind of MISTAKE! I had signed up for PHOTO LAYOUT ARTIST!

And Brandon was supposed to be <u>MY</u> MENTOR!!

I was not at all surprised to see MacKenzie staring at me from across the room with this little smirk on her face. I wanted to walk over and slap it right off her—

OMG! I've been SO distracted writing about that crazy newspaper meeting that I haven't heard a single word my geometry teacher has said. . .

<u>Wait a minute. . .</u> !! Did he just tell us to clear our desks?!!!

Because we're having a POP QUIZ?!!!!!

RIGHT NOW?! NOOOOOOO!!!

"What makes up an IRREGULAR quadrilateral?"

Um, how about CONSTIPATED quadrangles?!

Heck if I know!

I'm so going to fail this quiz.

Then my parents are going to do something completely crazy and irrational like take away my phone.

Somebody PLEASE help me. . .

☹!!

OMG! That meeting was a disaster!

In just thirty minutes my newspaper adventure had gone from a dream come true to a total nightmare.

"Okay, now that everyone's been assigned a partner, any questions?" Zimmerman asked as the room started to buzz with excitement.

"Uh, Mr Zimmerman. . ."

I tried talking a little louder.

"Excuse me, but I think you forgot m—"

"Just work closely with your mentor. And most important, DON'T SCREW UP MY NEWSPAPER!" he yelled.

In spite of the fact that I was waving my hand frantically, he looked right past me like I was invisible.

Then he started muttering. . .

ME →

WAIT A MINUTE! I THINK I
LEFT MY BROWN SOCKS IN
THE DRYER! OR WAS IT THE
MICROWAVE?!

Then Zimmerman walked to his desk, collapsed in his
chair and started munching on sweets again.

Everyone else was busy working. But I just sat there like an idiot with no clue what to do.

OPTION 1:

Go up to Zimmerman and tell him he forgot to assign me a position.

Even though I was afraid he'd lose his temper and munch on my head like one of those sweet thingies for disturbing him.

OPTION 2:

Stay seated, smile mindlessly and fiddle with my pen until the hour was over.

Then find a secluded place and CRY like a BABY!

OPTION 3:

Pull a Zimmerman. Climb on top of my desk and yell at the top of my lungs like a maniac . . .

YOU FORGOT ME!!

However, since I'm actually a very shy person, I was leaning more toward Option 2.

I was trying to blink back tears of frustration when Brandon came over.

He gave me a warm smile.

"Welcome to the wacky world of newspaper! So, how's it going? I take it you decided against the photo layout artist position? I'm sure you'll like being an assistant editor."

"Um, actually, I didn't get an assignment at all. I think Zimmerman forgot me or something." The lump in my throat was so big, I could barely speak.

I guess that's when Brandon finally realised something was wrong.

Because suddenly his smile vanished and he kind of stared at me with this really concerned look on his face.

UM . . . NIKKI, ARE YOU OKAY?

"I guess I should have warned you about Zimmerman before you signed up. He's not so bad once you get to know him. But sometimes he can be a little. . ."

Brandon made a face and glanced at our teacher to see if he was listening. But Mr Zimmerman was oblivious, busily reloading his Scooby-Doo PEZ dispenser.

". . . well, scatterbrained!"

Brandon's mouth whispered "scatterbrained," but his eyes screamed "PSYCHOPATH!!"

"You should let him know you haven't been assigned anything yet. If you don't feel comfortable, I'll tell him for you. I know he can be a little intimidating. . ."

"BRANDON! BRANDON!" Across the room his partner, Britney, was screaming like her hair was on fire. MacKenzie stood close by, whispering to her.

But Brandon totally ignored her.

"Looks like your mentee is in desperate need of some, um . . . mentoring," I said, rolling my eyes. "Listen, I really appreciate your offer, but I can talk to Zimmerman myself."

The last thing I wanted was for Brandon to ~~know~~ THINK I was a wimp and too scared to go up and talk to the teacher.

I mean, how juvenile would THAT be?! Especially since Brandon and MacKenzie actually liked the guy.

"Well, let me know if I can help out, okay?"

He hesitated for a moment, hoping I would change my mind. Then he shrugged and walked back over to his partner.

After giving myself a ten-minute pep talk, I finally gathered enough courage to approach Zimmerman's desk.

I stood in front of him for what seemed like forever, waiting for him to notice me.

But he just typed away on his laptop without looking up.

I cleared my throat and plastered a fake smile on my face. "HI, THERE!" I croaked. My voice came out way louder than I anticipated.

Mr Zimmerman cringed like I had just shattered a glass, then looked up at me.

"How can I help you, Sparky?" he said sarcastically.

Now that I had his attention, I totally lost my nerve. I opened my mouth but no sound came out.

"WHAT?!" he exclaimed, rolling his eyes. Then he whispered, "So . . . are you trying to communicate with me telepathically?"

That's when I totally panicked. "Um . . . can I go to the toilet?" I blurted out.

"Go ahead." He frowned. "You don't need my permission for that. Now SHOO! I'm very busy!"

"Um, okay, thanks. . ."

As I turned to run from the room, I just barely missed stumbling over the bin.

"Excuse me!" I said.

I don't normally make it a habit to talk to inanimate objects.

But right then I was a nervous wreck!

That's when I noticed the sign-up sheet inside.

And what looked like a crossed-out name.

I peeked at Zimmerman and wondered if he'd have a hissy fit if he saw me rummaging through his trash.

But he had resumed typing and didn't seem to notice I was still standing there.

Finally my curiosity got the best of me. I bent down and grabbed the sign-up sheet. . .

I took one look at it and gasped. Suddenly
everything made sense!

WCD
NEWS

SIGN-UP SHEET FOR NEW MEMBERS

POSITION	NAME
ASSISTANT NEWS EDITOR	ALEX WESTLAKE
ASSISTANT FASHION EDITOR	Marcy Simms
ASSISTANT MOVIE REVIEWER	Chase Barrymore
~~PHOTO LAYOUT ARTIST~~	~~Nikki Maxwell~~
ASSISTANT COMICS PANELIST	Brian Lopez
ASSISTANT SPORTS EDITOR	Justin Smith
Photo Layout Artist	Britney Chung

WCD NEWS:
"THE WHEN, WHAT, WHERE AND WHY OF WCD!"

SOMEONE HAD CROSSED MY NAME OFF THE
SIGN-UP SHEET!!

And there was no doubt WHATSOEVER in my mind
that the dirty, stinkin' RAT was:

MACKENZIE ☹!!

So that's why I wasn't assigned a partner!

All I had to do now was explain to Zimmerman that
my name had somehow been "accidentally" crossed
out and then ~~ask~~ BEG him for a position.

I'd take just about anything.

Even . . . fashion.

Mostly because I needed to keep an eye on
MacKenzie. Really badly!

I smoothed out the sheet and walked back to
Zimmerman's desk.

"Um, excuse me, I really hate to bother you again,
Mr Zimmerman, but something's wrong—"

"I *TOTALLY* agree with you!" he said, closing his eyes and rubbing his temples.

"You do?" I was starting to think maybe this guy wasn't so bad after all.

"YOU'RE supposed to be in the TOILET. But for some strange reason you're STILL standing here PESTERING me. That's just . . . WRONG!"

"Well, actually, I was on my way to the girls' toilets. But then I saw our sign-up sheet and—"

"Really?! How'd our sign-up sheet get in the girls' toilets?"

"Um, actually, it wasn't IN the—"

"Listen! I'm REALLY busy right now! I suggest you go back to the toilets and just try to ignore that sign-up sheet in there. It probably won't hurt you. Okay!"

"I'm sorry for making all of this is so confusing. But somehow my name got crossed off of the sign-up sheet. Everyone got assigned a position on the newspaper staff except—"

Suddenly Zimmerman's mobile phone rang.

He answered it and held up a finger to shush me.

I could NOT believe that man actually had the nerve to SHUSH me right to my face like that! I was SO mad I wanted to just, um . . . SPIT!!

"Zimmerman here. No, never! I'll go to jail before I reveal my source."

He grabbed the papers off his desk and began stuffing them into his already overflowing bag while yelling into the phone. "And just for the record, I have no idea how my socks got inside that microwave. . . !"

As he hurried away, I anxiously chased after him.

ME, CHASING MR ZIMMERMAN!!

I had finally caught up with him and was just about to show him the sign-up sheet when . . .

SLAM!

That was the sound of the door he slammed right in my face as he rushed out of the classroom.

I just stood there blinking my eyes with the sign-up sheet dangling in my hand.

I looked around the room for help, but everyone was busily working with their partners on their projects.

Well, everyone except MacKenzie.

I could feel her beady little eyes staring at me from across the room.

But I didn't care anymore!

I'd had quite enough of the newspaper, thank you!

I grabbed my notepad and pen and was about to leave when she sashayed over.

LEAVING SO SOON?

But I didn't say a word. I just walked right past her.

"Well, it looks like YOUR day was a total waste of makeup," she snarled. "TOO BAD!"

I couldn't believe MacKenzie had so coldly and

cruelly crushed all of my hopes and dreams beneath the bloodred sole of her designer shoe.

That girl is beyond RUTHLESS!

First she UNDERMINED my WCD scholarship by convincing HER dad to offer MY dad a job at Hollister Holdings, Inc.

And now she's UNDERMINED my plan for getting on the school newspaper by crossing my name off the sign-up sheet.

What am I going to do now?!

My life is HOPELESS!!

☹!!

THURSDAY, JANUARY 16

All day I've been depressed and feeling like a complete and utter FAILURE.

After that mental BEATDOWN by MacKenzie during the newspaper meeting, my self-esteem is pretty much pulverised.

Chloe and Zoey must have sensed I was really down in the dumps.

Because during our library session they kept needling me about WHY I had changed my mind about joining the newspaper staff.

FINALLY I broke down and told them the truth. Well, part of the truth, anyway.

MacKenzie had single-handedly got me kicked out before I'd even had a chance to get in.

And Zimmerman was a certified LOONEY TUNE!

Well, Chloe and Zoey weren't having it. And boy, were those two totally ticked off!

NUH-UH! We're NOT going to just stand by and let our kind, but socially challenged, BFF be picked on and treated like a snivelling pushover by some egotistical, fashion-obsessed diva.

Sorry, girlfriend! But even insecure scaredy-pants with low self-esteem totally deserve to be treated with kindness and respect, Nikki!

I just stared at them in disbelief! I could not believe they had actually said all of that stuff.

OMG! Those were two of the nicest compliments I'd EVER received in my entire LIFE.

I do not deserve friends like Chloe and Zoey.

They're, like, the BEST friends EVER!

They marched me right over to Zimmerman's classroom.

Then they both looked me in the eye and said if I didn't get in there and demand a position on the newspaper, they were going to kick my BUTT.

It was SO funny. Because of course they were joking.

I think.

As I stood outside Zimmerman's door, it was reassuring to know my BFFs had my back and were there gently cheering me on. . .

OMG! I was so nervous I was practically shaking. I felt like I was Dorothy going to visit that scary Wizard of Oz guy or something.

When Zimmerman saw me walk in, he just muttered,
"So, I hope you finally made it to the toilets. . ."

"Actually, I didn't. I'm here because you missed me

when you assigned jobs at the last newspaper meeting. Somehow my name got accidentally crossed off the list or something. See, it's right here. . ." I handed him the paper.

"Is that so?" Zimmerman read it over and then glanced up at the board. "Looks like you're right. The only problem is there's no more room for you. I had two additional people join yesterday. And I made them Lauren's assistants. Now maybe she'll be able to get my coffee to me before it gets cold."

"There HAS to be something I can do!" I pleaded. "To be honest, I have this big problem, and the only way I can straighten it out is to get on the newspaper staff. My friends are counting on me and I don't want to let them down. PLEASE!"

"Hey, slow your roll, kiddo! I feel your pain. But I'm really sorry. . ."

Zimmerman popped three sweets into his mouth and munched on them loudly while checking his watch.

I could not believe this guy!

What a cruddy teacher! I had come to him with a problem, and he had the nerve to just sit there and ignore me like I was one of his empty coffee cups. . .

ME →

ME, AS ONE OF THE PAPER CUPS LITTERING
MR. ZIMMERMAN'S OFFICE

"Well, thanks for talking to me." I sighed loudly and turned to leave as I blinked back a wave of tears.

Zimmerman suddenly leaned back in his chair, stared into space and scratched his fuzzy chin.

"Hold on! I might have something for you, Sparky. But it's going to be a lot of work. We're going to bring back the WCD advice column. Just for you!"

"Advice column? Just for m—me?" I stammered. My anger melted and was quickly replaced by raging insecurity. I was back to a sniveling rookie. "You mean, I'll be doing this all alone? With no mentor?"

"That's right," he answered. "I have a feeling you have the spunk to pull it off. Either that, or you'll single-handedly destroy the newspaper's reputation and give me a heart attack. But you wouldn't do that to me, would you, Sparky?"

"Well, I dunno. . ." I gulped.

"Of course you wouldn't!"

"I'm not that good at dishing out advice. What if kids don't like my answers? They might get mad at me and say nasty things."

"There's always that possibility. So when you write, you might want to use a pseudonym."

"Um, okay. But I don't think I have one. Is that like a computer?"

Zimmerman chuckled. "Sparky, you remind me a lot of myself when I was just getting started. Not much knowledge, but a lot of heart. Nope, it's not a computer. It's just a pen name."

"Oh, I get it! Pseudonym is a brand of ink pens."

Zimmerman looked annoyed and popped two sweets into his mouth.

"Okay, let's start over. Now, pay close attention, Sparky. 'Pseudonym' is just a fancy word for writing with a phony name. You know, so your readers won't harass you, hunt you down, or send you gross stuff in the mail. You'd NEVER believe the stuff I've got in the mail from disgruntled readers. Of course Lauren and I will keep your identity a secret, and we'll tell the staff you're our new assistant."

"Oh! Now I understand. I'll need to make up a catchy name."

"Exactly! See that bottom drawer of my file cabinet? Your stuff will be under lock and key in a black metal box. Check there tomorrow morning and you'll find everything you need to get started."

"Thanks, Mr Zimmerman. You have no idea how much this means to—"

"Now get out of my classroom. I have something important to do. SpongeBob comes on in two minutes. You know, he's the last Great American Hero." He waved his hand to shoo me away. "Good luck, kiddo."

His Royal KOOKINESS had spoken!

Starting tomorrow, I was going to become the WCD

version of Dr Phil. But with hoop earrings, lip gloss, a few pimples and, most dangerously, no experience WHATSOEVER.

And if I screwed it up, it was gonna be . . .

OFF WITH MY HEAD!

MY HEAD →

I was SO excited, I did my Snoopy "happy dance" all the way back to the library.

Chloe and Zoey are going to be superproud of me.

Am I qualified to give advice to my peers? Of course not! I can't even decide on milk or OJ in the morning.

But when my gut tells me something, it's usually right. So I'll do my very best to help people NOT mess up their lives. Guts, don't fail me now!!

Eww . . . that sounded kinda gross, didn't it?

Anyway, I'm about to make a major comeback!

And not even the evil forces of the DIVA OF DOOM (also known as MacKenzie) can stop me.

☺!!

Today was officially my first day on the job as a
staff writer for the WCD newspaper as my advice
expert alter ego, Miss Know-It-All.

Mr Zimmerman made an announcement over the
school PA system yesterday about the return of the
advice column and instructed students to leave their
letters to Miss Know-It-All in a special mailbox
outside the newspaper room.

I couldn't wait to see how many letters I'd got. For
once in my life, I was out of bed BEFORE my alarm
clock went off.

I hopped into the shower, brushed my teeth and
threw on some clothes. Then I ran to the kitchen to
grab a granola bar for breakfast.

"Good morning, dear!" Mom smiled. "Up already?"

"Yep," I said, shoving the granola bar into my mouth.
"I'm working on a newspaper project! Mom, do you

think you could take me to school extra early?"

When I got to the newspaper room, Lauren was busy reading over both the print and online versions of the school paper before they were released for publication.

All newspaper staff had access to them too, which very conveniently allowed me to monitor MacKenzie's Fashion and Current Events column.

If she tried to publish anything untrue about me or my friends, I'd report her to Zimmerman so fast it would make her head spin.

"Good morning!" I said cheerfully. "I'm ready to get started on my advice column. What does my mail look like?"

"Hi, Nikki! Well, let's check your mailbox," Lauren said as she picked up a metal box right outside the door and set it on her desk.

The box was covered with a thick layer of dust.

155

"It looks like this thing hasn't been used in years!" she said as she brushed her dusty hands on her pants and unlocked the box with a key.

My heart pounded as I waited to see how many letters I'd got — ten, twenty, maybe even fifty. But it dropped when I saw what students had left for me in the box. . .

"OMG!" I gasped as I stared in disbelief at a broken pencil, a sweet wrapper, a wad of gum and a used tissue.

"Gross! Some kids are SO immature!" I fumed, trying to pretend I wasn't as disappointed as I felt. "This is NOT a rubbish bin!"

"I'm sorry," Lauren said. "But our reader feedback has been almost nonexistent. We're hoping your column will change things. But it looks like the paper is going to take some time to catch on."

I didn't want to say it, but I was worried our paper would never "catch on". Other than Brandon's amazing photographs, the articles were dullsville.

The one time I did read an issue, there was a page-long interview with the lunch lady on nutrition. Yawn!

First of all, how exciting could her interview be? Second, what would she know about nutrition, serving us imitation ham on a mouldy roll?

After Lauren left the room, I collapsed in a chair and blinked back my tears. I felt as worthless as that rubbish in my advice box ☹!

I decided to update Chloe and Zoey by text: "Bad news!! My Miss Know-It-All advice column was a total FLOP! No letters, just rubbish!"

I got the exact same text from both of them: "☹!"

I sighed and tried to swallow the huge lump in my throat.

At some point I was going to have to tell them the truth.

MacKenzie was going to make sure we were suspended from school for the Great Toilet Paper Caper and for egging her house unless WE convinced Brandon to invite MacKenzie and Jessica to his party.

Who would have guessed that MacKenzie's diverse talents include a keen fashion sense, pathological lying and blackmailing?

That girl was basically a middle school mafioso in lip gloss and hoop earrings.

It was quite obvious she really, really liked attending parties.

That's when I got a text from Chloe to Zoey and me: "Just finished COOLEST book ever. Shy girl decides to run for student council president and her opponent/crush becomes her campaign manager."

I knew Chloe LOVED to read, but I was in the middle of a MAJOR life crisis! For once, couldn't she just try focusing on ME instead of her stupid book characters?!

Then Chloe sent us both a third text: "Snarfing down breakfast. Zoey, call me right NOW! Nikki, meet us in the library in fifteen minutes!"

Just GREAT ☹!

Like I wanted to start off my disastrous morning sitting in the library listening to Chloe gush over yet another of her teen romance novels.

I was already in the library sulking and having a pity party for myself when Zoey arrived loaded down with empty shoe boxes and poster paper.

Chloe was not far behind, lugging a big bag stuffed with scissors, glue, paper, paint and glitter.

"What's g-going on?" I sniffed sadly.

"We're here to save our FAVE advice columnist, Miss Know-It-All. . ." Chloe explained excitedly, and gave me jazz hands.

"We came up with the idea of putting up posters with supercute help boxes all around the school," Zoey said. "So . . . what do you think?"

"I THINK . . . you guys are AWESOME!" I squealed.

Then I watched in amazement as my BFFs worked their magic with glitter and glue. . .

Thanks to Chloe and Zoey, I now have four fabulously cool posters with help boxes AND a catchy new slogan.

Luckily, we managed to get everything done and posted in the hallways just before students started to arrive for class. . .

One thing is for certain, Chloe and Zoey's chic marketing campaign for Miss Know-It-All really created a buzz.

By lunchtime, the ENTIRE school was gossiping about it.

And since the identity of Miss Know-It-All is a big secret, everyone was trying to guess who she was.

Not a single person would EVER suspect it was ME!

I just hope I start getting letters really soon.

Because if Mr Zimmerman cancels the advice column again due to lack of interest, I won't be able to stop MacKenzie from printing her pack of lies in the school newspaper, and we could all end up KICKED OUT OF SCHOOL!

!!

SATURDAY, JANUARY 18

ARGH!!

I feel just like I'm back in Madame Fufu's beginning dance class again!

WHY?!

Because Brianna's dance school is having its annual fund-raiser to pay for all of those frilly little dance costumes they wear for recitals.

Each student has to sell sixty shocolate bars.

At first I felt kind of sorry for her.

Until my parents told me I had to go door-to-door in our neighbourhood to help Brianna and keep an eye on her. Now I feel sorry for ME!

"Hey! Why do I have to sell chocolate?" I grumped. "I don't need a frilly little dance costume!"

ME, WEARING A FRILLY BALLET COSTUME
THAT I *DON'T NEED* FOR A CLASS I'M *NOT IN*

But I guess they didn't understand my logic.

"What's a fundraiser?" Brianna asked as we trudged
through the snow in our driveway.

"It's what we're doing right now," I muttered.

I was exhausted, and I hadn't even made it out of our front garden yet.

Those two bags of chocolate bars seemed to weigh fifty kilograms each.

I started to wonder if each bar was actually filled with a nutty caramel centre or CEMENT.

"I don't get it!" Brianna said.

I sighed. "A fundraiser is when you sell stuff to get money for something important."

"We're going to get MONEY for these chocolate bars?!" Brianna exclaimed. "Goody gumdrops! I'm gonna use my money to buy me a baby unicorn!"

"No! You DON'T get to keep it. You have to give it to your dance school.

"That's not fair! Why should I sell stuff if I can't keep the money?" Brianna complained.

"Just . . . because! You're asking too many questions. Let's walk over to the next street so no one I know will see us — I mean, so we can cover more ground."

I rang the doorbell of the first house on the street.

"Just let me do the talking, okay, Brianna?"

"But they're MY chocolate bars!" she shot back. "You're NOT the boss of me!"

"You'll only mess things up! Just keep quiet so we can sell this junk to some unsuspecting fools and go home!" I yelled at her.

"Uh . . . can I help you?"

Brianna and I both jumped. A man was standing at the door in exercise gear that was way too tight around his stomach.

We hadn't noticed him there while we were fighting. He had an irritated frown on his face.

"Oh, sorry!" I cleared my throat. "Actually, we're here to see if you would be interested in buying a delicious gourmet chocolate bar to support fine arts for children. It's only three dollars."

"Only three dollars?" The man laughed sarcastically. "You must think I'M some unsuspecting FOOL! No thanks. Besides, I'm on a strict diet . . . unless you're selling dark chocolate. . ."

"Actually, we are!" I said as I smiled and held up two bars. "Would you like the one with nuts or the one without nu—"

That's when Brianna rudely interrupted my sales pitch.

"WOW!! YOUR BELLY JIGGLES JUST LIKE SANTA CLAUS! ARE YOU GUYS RELATED?" she blurted out.

The man glared at us and turned bright red.

Then he said some not-so-nice words and slammed the door right in our faces!

169

"Brianna! Why did you have to open your big mouth?" I scolded. "Look what you did!"

"It was a compliment! Why'd he get so mad?" she asked, scratching her head.

Sometimes I wonder if Brianna is really that naive. Or does she just enjoy aggravating me in the hope that one day I'll burst an artery and drop DEAD so she can get my bedroom and new phone?

"Forget it!" I said, and took a deep breath to calm myself down. "Let's just go to the next house."

We went to another six houses and still no luck. Since it was starting to snow, I decided to call it a day and just go home.

Which was the smart thing to do, considering the fact that my toes and those stupid chocolate bars were pretty much frozen solid and liable to snap into little pieces at the slightest touch.

☹!!

Since Brianna didn't sell a single chocolate bar yesterday, my mom insisted that we go back out again after we got home from church.

I was like, JUST GREAT ☹!!

When we got to the first house, I rang the doorbell.

"Keep quiet. Got it?!" I whispered to Brianna.

She nodded and pretended to zip her mouth closed.

The door slowly opened, and a skinny old lady with no teeth stood there scowling at us.

At least, I thought it was a scowl.

But I really couldn't tell because her mouth looked all sunken in, like she had just sucked on a lemon or something. . .

"Um, good afternoon, ma'am," I began awkwardly.
"We were wondering if you would like to support
fine arts for children by purchasing a chocolate—"

"SIC 'EM, TATER TOT!"

the woman yelled at the top of her lungs.

Brianna and I looked behind her, expecting to see a

giant Doberman with one of those collars with spikes on it.

Instead, a fat white cat with a pink bow poked its head out and glared at us.

MEEEOOOWWW!!!

Then Tater Tot hissed, snarled and charged.

Brianna and I turned around and ran for our lives, screaming.

YOWL!!

AAAHH!

AAAHH!

YUM-TUMS

YUM-TUMS

← BRIANNA AND I RUN FOR OUR LIVES!

That cat probably chased us down the entire street. Although I wasn't exactly sure because I didn't dare look behind me.

Hey! Chubby cats are no joke! Especially when they're angry!

If you'd seen that crazy look in Tater Tot's eyes, you would have run for your life TOO!

Finally Brianna and I collapsed on a snowbank and lay there, trying to catch our breath.

"I don't . . . wanna . . . do this . . . anymore!" Brianna panted.

"Me . . . neither!" I huffed in response.

"Excuse me," said a voice from the pavement.

My body was paralysed with exhaustion, so I just lifted my head. A confused-looking bus driver stood above us, fiddling with her GPS.

"Sorry to trouble you, but I can't get this darn GPS to work! Can you tell me where the nearest petrol station is?" she asked.

"Sure," I answered, forcing my tired lips to move. "Just go down this street about a mile. It will be on the corner on the right."

Then I lifted my weary arm and pointed north.

"Thanks a million, hon." Suddenly the bus driver's eyes lit up. "Hey! Are those chocolate bars?"

"Um . . . yeah," I answered.

"Can I buy one from you? I'm starving!"

"You actually wanna buy one of these?" I asked, surprised. "Okay! We have an assortment of—"

"Hey, lady!" Brianna interrupted. "My sister says we're only supposed to be selling these to unsuspecting fools. But you kind of look like one to me. . ."

The bus driver lady gave us $3.00 and Brianna grabbed a chocolate bar and handed it to her.

BRIANNA AND I *FINALLY* SELL A
STUPID CHOCOLATE BAR!

She tore off the wrapper and took a big bite.

"Wow! This is really good!" she exclaimed.

"I need to get rid of all of these guys! Do you want to buy fifty-nine more?" Brianna asked hopefully.

"I don't think so, sweetheart," the lady chuckled. "But I've got a good idea. Why don't you offer them to the passengers on my bus? They're on their way to the Westchester Hills weight-loss camp."

"Really?! Are you sure that won't be too much trouble?" I asked.

"Hey! They've been snacking on carrots, celery and water for the past three hours and could probably use some real food. Assuming, of course, they haven't morphed into rabbits and hopped off my bus by now!" She laughed and winked at us.

Brianna and I grinned from ear to ear. We were starting to think that maybe we'd hit the jackpot!

"Okay!" we said, and grabbed our bags of chocolate.

OMG! It was a CHOCOLATE MASSACRE on that bus!

People were screaming and waving money in the air
as they climbed over each other to get to us.

Then they bought two or three bars each and gobbled them up like they hadn't had a crumb of food in days.

We sold Brianna's entire two bags in less than five minutes. I was SO relieved that chocolate fiasco was FINALLY over.

On our way home, Brianna and I started thinking. Maybe we could go into business together and get rich selling chocolate bars at weight-loss camps.

I'd use my money for WCD tuition, and Brianna said she'd buy a baby unicorn.

I seriously thought about telling her that unicorns don't exist. But then I decided, NAH!!

After we make our first million, I'll probably just pay for a really good therapist for her. I'm just sayin'!

☺!!

Today in gym class we started practising for the President's Challenge physical fitness test, which is given each spring.

To make sure students had adequate time to train, our gym teacher gave us a handout back in the autumn with the names of the four exercises we were going to be tested on: curl-ups, push-ups, pull-ups and crunches.

My health and fitness are VERY important to me. So I've been doing these exercises at home every day to try to stay in shape.

Unfortunately, I just found out today I was doing ALL of them totally WRONG ☹!!

I'm SO disgusted! This is all my teacher's fault. She should have provided specific instructions on HOW to DO these exercises.

Now I'm really worried that I'm going to completely FAIL the presidential fitness test. . .

EXERCISE #1: CURL-UPS

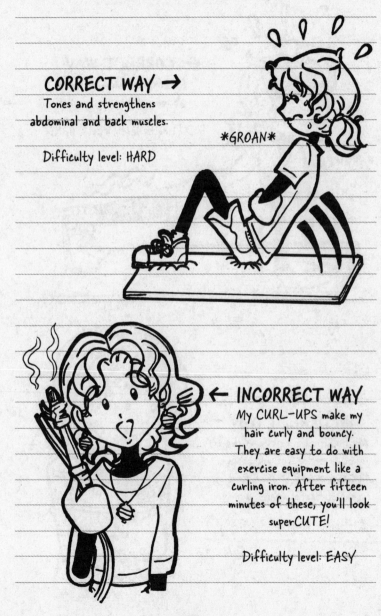

CORRECT WAY →
Tones and strengthens abdominal and back muscles.

Difficulty level: HARD

GROAN

← INCORRECT WAY
My CURL-UPS make my hair curly and bouncy. They are easy to do with exercise equipment like a curling iron. After fifteen minutes of these, you'll look superCUTE!

Difficulty level: EASY

EXERCISE #2: PUSH-UPS

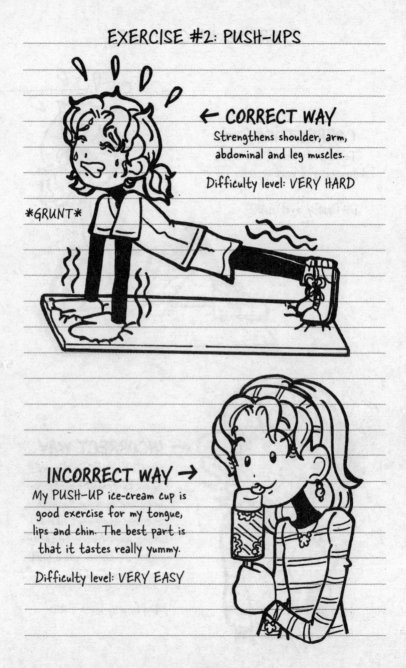

← **CORRECT WAY**
Strengthens shoulder, arm, abdominal and leg muscles.

Difficulty level: VERY HARD

GRUNT

INCORRECT WAY →
My PUSH-UP ice-cream cup is good exercise for my tongue, lips and chin. The best part is that it tastes really yummy.

Difficulty level: VERY EASY

EXERCISE #3: PULL-UPS

UGH

CORRECT WAY →
Strengthens and tones arm
and back muscles.

Difficulty level:
NEXT TO IMPOSSIBLE

← INCORRECT WAY
My PULL-UPS are great
for socks, pants, tights, gym
shorts and anything else that
has a tendency to fall down
around your ankles. It exercises
fingers and improves balance.

Difficulty level: EASY

EXERCISE #4: CRUNCHES

CORRECT WAY →

Tones and strengthens back, arm and abdominal muscles.

Difficulty level: HARD

MOAN

CRUNCH

← INCORRECT WAY

My CRUNCHES are fun and easy to do. I just bite down really hard on a yummy, crunchy snack like crisps, nachos, pretzels, or apples, then chew. This exercises my jaw muscles and teeth.

Difficulty level: EASY PEASY

See what I mean?! I've wasted a lot of time and energy doing the WRONG exercises.

I'm thinking about filing a petition with the school board, requesting that students be given the choice to do either version.

At least MY exercises aren't superHARD and they DON'T make you all sore, sweaty and smelly like the ones from that presidential fitness program.

Anyway, while I was in the locker room getting dressed after gym, I was really looking forward to checking my new help boxes after school today.

UNTIL I overheard MacKenzie and a few of the CCPs saying the advice column idea is SO LAME and that only a TOTAL LOSER would write in to Miss Know-It-All.

Now I'm SUPERworried they might be right.

Because between classes I couldn't help but notice everyone walking right past my help boxes, ignoring them.

To make matters worse, I'm in a really GRUMPY mood and in extreme PAIN from doing all of those really difficult exercises the CORRECT way.

I'm so stressed out that I decided to wait and check my help boxes tomorrow. Even though I already know they're probably going to be EMPTY.

Oh! I almost forgot! I got even MORE bad news when I got home from school.

It looks to me like my dad has decided to work full-time for Hollister Holdings, Inc.!

Earlier today, he actually put his work van up for sale at a used car dealership.

I can't BELIEVE he just dumped Max the Roach at some used car lot!

That's just . . . COLD!

At least Dad could have let us all say our goodbyes to him so we could have closure!

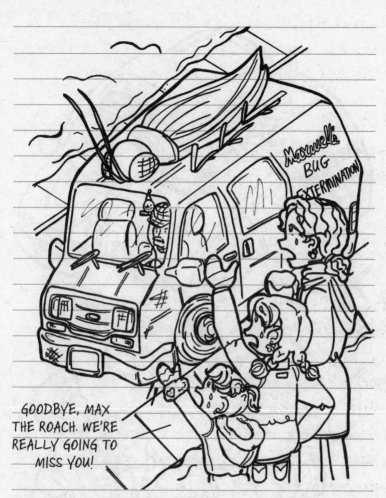

GOODBYE, MAX
THE ROACH. WE'RE
REALLY GOING TO
MISS YOU!

And I'm pretty sure Max is going to miss us, too! I bet he'll be really lonely at that big used car lot.

Especially with all of those total strangers very rudely GAWKING at him all day long. . .

TOTAL STRANGERS RUDELY GAWKING AT
MAX THE ROACH!

POOR MAX!! He's going to need some serious therapy when he gets older.

OMG! I just had the most horrifying thought!

What if AFTER MacKenzie's dad hired my dad full-time, she made him FIRE MY dad!!

Then not only would I lose my WCD scholarship, but my entire family could end up HOMELESS!

SORRY!! But I've got a really, really, really, really BAD feeling about Dad working for Hollister Holdings, Inc.

!!

All day I've been SUPERdepressed.

I'm absolutely DREADING having to check the Miss Know-It-All help boxes.

I'm sure Lauren has already told Mr Zimmerman that the ONLY thing students were leaving for me was rubbish.

My column is probably in danger of being cancelled, and I haven't even answered my first letter yet.

Anyway, by lunchtime I felt like crying AGAIN.

But I didn't because I knew everyone in the cafeteria was just going to stare and whisper.

Unfortunately, I couldn't avoid the inevitable.

So instead of going to the library to shelve books, I decided to hide out in the janitor's closet until all the students were in class and the halls were completely empty.

My heart was pounding as I took a deep breath and stared at the rainbow help box in the hall near my locker.

Then I slowly removed the top, and . . .

There were two letters inside ☺!!

OMG! I was SO relieved.

Then I raced down the hall to check the striped box right outside the cafeteria.

There was a letter in there, too!

And there was one letter in the smiley-face box near the drinking fountain and — get this — TWO letters in the metal box outside the newspaper room.

I couldn't believe it!

Chloe and Zoey's very chic marketing strategy had actually worked.

Miss Know-It-All had got a total of SIX letters requesting advice!

I was so happy I did my Snoopy "happy dance" right there in front of the girls' toliets.

Because those letters were MINE!

ALL MINE!!

Then, like the big dork that I am, I actually gave them all a very big HUG. . .

SQUEE!

ME, LOVING MY LETTERS!

Miss Know-It-All is officially in BUSINESS.

And MacKenzie had better watch her back ☺!!

I stayed after school to work on my first batch of Miss Know-It-All letters.

Dear Miss Know-It-All,

I don't normally do this sort of thing, 'cause I'll totally get called out for it. But here goes nothing. . .

I'm a popular guy and a star athlete and my girlfriend is a cute cheerleader. We have been together for two weeks. My life is pretty sweet, except that I keep my favourite hobby a huge secret from people because I am super embarrassed about it.

The truth is, I love to bake. After a gruelling day of football I like to just chill out and make red velvet cupcakes. One day my girlfriend almost caught me red-handed, but I lied and said my mom made them.

She said the cupcakes were the best she'd ever had. I want to tell her the truth, but I'm afraid she'll laugh and break up with me. What should I do?

-Cupcake Man

I suddenly remembered how shocked I was to find a cupcake cookbook in the boys' locker room when I was searching for my lost diary. The cookbook belonged to the football team captain, Brady Grayson.

194

"I can't believe he wrote this," I laughed to myself. "How adorable!"

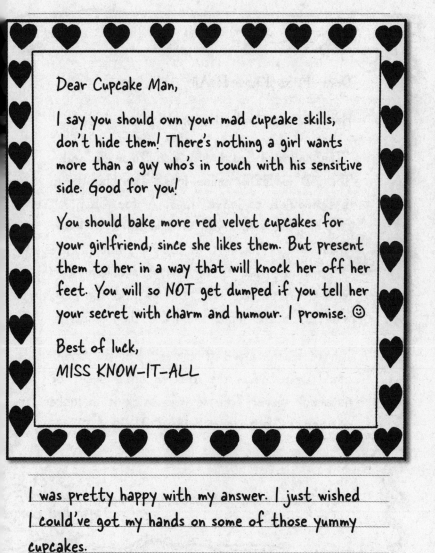

Dear Cupcake Man,

I say you should own your mad cupcake skills, don't hide them! There's nothing a girl wants more than a guy who's in touch with his sensitive side. Good for you!

You should bake more red velvet cupcakes for your girlfriend, since she likes them. But present them to her in a way that will knock her off her feet. You will so NOT get dumped if you tell her your secret with charm and humour. I promise. ☺

Best of luck,
MISS KNOW-IT-ALL

I was pretty happy with my answer. I just wished I could've got my hands on some of those yummy cupcakes.

The next letter was possibly a prank, but I
answered it anyway.

Dear Miss Know-It-All,

Help me out with this one!

"The railroad track between Town A and
Town B is 500 miles long. The blue train
is scheduled to leave Town A for Town B at
2 p.m. The red train is scheduled to leave
Town B for Town A at 3 p.m., but is delayed
95 minutes due to an engine problem. If the
blue train travels at 35 mph and the red train
travels at 50 mph, when will they meet?"

I hate maths word problems. Do you think you
could write down the answer on a sheet of
notebook paper for me and stick it in locker
number 108 before Friday? Thanks!

—Slacker Superstar

P.S. Make sure you show your work!

SLACKER
SUPERSTAR

A few of my brain cells died just reading that letter!

I figured Slacker Superstar would get a higher score on his/her homework turning in a paper with Brianna's drawing of a giraffe than with MY help.

But I wrote my answer down on paper and stuck it in locker 108 as instructed.

Dear Slacker Superstar,

It took me a while, but I finally solved your very complicated math problem.

Here is the answer:

DO YOUR OWN HOMEWORK! And if you need help, try getting a maths tutor.

Best of luck,
MISS KNOW-IT-ALL

P.S. Please make sure you show YOUR work!

This next letter could have been written by me.

I guess I'm NOT the only older sister with a bratty little sister or brother who drives her totally nuts!

Dear Miss Know-It-All,

I have a little brother who drives me absolutely CRAZY! He's always getting into my stuff, embarrassing me in public and reading my diary. But that's not the worst of it.

Whenever I'm forced to babysit him, something gets shattered into tiny pieces, eaten (including my homework), or burns to the ground.

My parents always chew me out and tell me I need to take charge as his babysitter, but he won't do anything I tell him.

How do I keep my sanity and control a wild six-year-old?

—Big Sister Blues

I really need to follow my OWN advice on this one:

Dear Big Sister Blues,

You have my deepest sympathy! I know how you feel because I have a sister just like that at home. All I can suggest is taking two paracetamol before babysitting and keeping the fire department on speed dial.

To be honest, I really don't know how to deal with younger siblings either. You don't need Miss Know-It-All's help! You need an animal trainer! And when you find one who doesn't run away screaming, would you do me a huge favour and give me his number?

Thanks,
MISS KNOW-IT-ALL

This next letter was a very deep and complex question most students ponder at some point in their lives. But it will forever remain unanswered. . .

Dear Miss Know-It-All,

What's in the meat loaf in the school cafeteria?

—Just Curious

Dear Just Curious,

Have you ever wondered why that month-old piece of meat loaf lying next to the bins outside has never turned green? Ever asked yourself where all the chemicals go after you do lab experiments in science class? I'm just sayin'! Not trying to put any of our lovely cafeteria staff on blast, but that meat is probably injected with more preservatives than Madonna's face! But let's look at the positive side. If you eat it, you probably won't look a day over thirteen years old when you graduate from college.

Bon appetit,
MISS KNOW-IT-ALL

Dear Miss Know-It-All,

Do girls really dig a guy who wears Buff Body cologne?

'Cause the commercial says supermodels will fall in love with you if you buy it, and that would totally rock!

—Desperate Dude

Dear Desperate Dude,

I'm just shakin' my head at this one. Commercials for boys are, by far, full of the most baloney I've ever seen. Those people are just taking you for a ride, Dude. If you had to choose between wearing Buff Body cologne or bug spray, PLEASE drench yourself in the bug spray! Buff Body reeks! Period.

Don't waste your money! Girls will be happy if you just shower every day. Besides, we tend to fall in love with our hearts, not our noses. It's just that simple.

Your friend,
MISS KNOW-IT-ALL

Dear Miss Know-It-All,

I'm crushing on my Hollywood idol, and some people think I'm obsessed. Who isn't crazy about him? He's only perfect, amazing, talented and SUPERcute!! I have all of his music and movies, millions of posters and every piece of fangirl merchandise out there. I'm president of his official fan club, so nobody knows him better than I do. And nobody's more perfect for him than I am!

My friends don't understand me either. At school, there's a guy named Alex who, I guess, kind of likes me. But I'm not interested because there's only one boy for me. My friends tell me I'm nuts for rejecting Alex, and that I need to get in touch with reality. But I just know that my dream guy and I are meant to be! Is it so wrong to be in love??

—Starstruck

Wow! Starstruck actually seemed to be really, really, um . . . starstruck! But who hasn't been in love with that supercute guy on the cover of your fave CD or starring in your fave teen sitcom? I decided to tell her the truth very gently.

Dear Starstruck,

There's nothing wrong with being in love, but sometimes people can mistake infatuation for love. You may think you know your idol because you've read about him. But you don't "know him", know him. Know what I mean? Sure, any girl would give her right arm to date him! But all they see is his celebrity image, not the real him. BTW . . . isn't he going steady with that cute Disney actress?! I don't think you need to give up being a fan, but why not crush on that nice guy in your maths class who makes you laugh? Love has a way of showing up where you least expect it!

Your friend,
MISS KNOW-IT-ALL

I can hardly believe that when the next newspaper comes out tomorrow, I will kinda, sorta be a published writer!

Wow! Mom is going to be so proud that she'll put my first column on the refrigerator next to one of Brianna's crazy drawings.

Hey, I'm just getting warmed up with this advice stuff.

But THIS is the totally mind-blowing part. . .

On my way out of the building, I checked all of my help boxes, and I'D GOT FOURTEEN MORE LETTERS!

SQUEEE!! Can you believe THAT?!!

So I'm going to wrap up this diary entry and get busy saving the world.

Miss Know-It-All's work is NEVER done!

☺!!

"Dear Miss Know-It-All."

I read the bold print at the top of my column over and over again. It felt like I was looking at an official article written by an official writer, who wasn't me. But it WAS me!

In the cafeteria, EVERYONE had their newspapers out, and they were reading my advice column on page 2.

"Have you seen 'Miss Know-It-All'?" Alexis, a cheerleader, asked her friend Samantha.

"I'm looking at it right now," she answered.

"Someone on our squad is dating a total sweetheart who loves to BAKE!" Alexis gushed. "How romantic is THAT?! And Miss Know-It-All gave him great advice! I SO envy his girlfriend!"

I just stood there in shock, listening to all of the chatter with a freakishly huge grin on my face.

ME, SHOCKED AND SURPRISED THAT
EVERYONE IS READING MISS KNOW-IT-ALL

But I couldn't just stand there basking in my
success. I had work to do.

Out of my twenty-one new letters, this one caught my eye:

Dear Miss Know-It-All,

I'm a well-liked teacher who has been with WCD for over fifteen years. I would say I'm a fairly easy person to get along with. But for whatever reason, another teacher has it in for me! Sometimes I come to class and my whiteboard erasers are missing. This forces me to use my hand or sleeve to erase the board, and by the end of the day, I'm a rainbow-coloured mess. Then, in the hall, I hear other teachers snickering at me, which is humiliating.

To make matters worse, this crook also steals my lunch from the teachers' lounge. I can't teach on an empty stomach! But it's either that or buy food from the cafeteria, and that's not happening. Do you know what they put in that stuff??

Anyway, I need your help. How do I find out who is doing this to me and get the respect I deserve?

—Taunted Teacher

You learn something new every day! I had no idea that teachers had a pecking order just like kids. But whoever that person was, my heart went out to him/her. I was eager to help my elder dork outsmart this overgrown bully.

Dear Taunted Teacher,

Sheesh! Anyone who'd resort to stealing sandwiches from fellow teachers needs to get a life! And most importantly, a loaf of bread, some mayo and ham.

I know a thing or two about bullying, and it stinks. But you have to fight brawn with brain. Wouldn't it be funny if a certain someone packed a "special" lunch of baked beans, prune juice and bran, so when a certain thief ate a stolen lunch, a certain surprise would make their crime obvious? The good news is that the culprit would NEVER mess with you again. The bad news is that you'd NEVER be able to use the toilet in the teachers' lounge again either! Consider it a minor casualty of war. I'm rooting for you!

Your friend,
MISS KNOW-IT-ALL

I was really anxious to see how that situation worked out. If any of the teachers were replaced by a substitute in the middle of the day, I'd know they were suffering from "the chocolate pudding of wrath". (Wink, wink!)

Normally, I would never promote revenge. And yes, I SO regret the Great Toilet Paper Caper. Everyone knows I'm basically a peaceful, fun-loving, Disney-watching hippie!

But if someone stole food out of my mouth, I'd be taking OFF my earrings and putting ON my boxing gloves. I'm just sayin'!

Anyway, as lunch was ending, I noticed a huge commotion in the hallway. The cheerleaders were crowded around a locker, and I could see Brady Grayson with a coy smile on his face.

"Brady! OMG!" squealed a cheerleader in pigtails.

I buried my face in my maths book like I was totally engaged in it (yeah, right!) so I could get closer and sneak a peek at what was going on.

Brady had decorated his girlfriend's locker with red wrapping paper and ribbon to make it look like a giant gift. And when she opened it, everyone gasped, including ME. . .

Brady had followed Miss Know-It-All's advice, and her locker was filled with red roses and red velvet cupcakes. He'd even spelled out "You're Special!" with alphabet magnets.

"I have a confession to make." Brady blushed. "I made those cupcakes you like, not my mom. I love baking, and I hope that doesn't change anything between us."

"Oh, Brady! Don't be silly!" she gushed as she gave him a big bear hug.

There wasn't a dry eye in the crowd. I could barely keep myself together. I buried my face deeper in my maths book so no one could see where those crazy-sounding sniffle-hiccups were coming from.

I was so proud of myself, and Brady, too. With a little sound advice, Prince CHUMP had become Prince CHARMING!

And at that moment just a teeny-tiny part of me was SUPERenvious of Brady's girlfriend. But not for long, because Miss Know-It-All's advice blew up in my face! Later that day I received a letter that sounded like it was written by his girlfriend.

Dear Miss Know-It-All,

I didn't think my boyfriend had a romantic bone in his body. He never talked about his feelings and he acted like he was too macho to do anything nice for me. But today he surprised me by filling my locker with roses and my favourite cupcakes!

My big problem now is that the entire cheerleading squad is crushing on MY boyfriend! I have to beat them off with a stick. I admit, I'm jealous of the attention he's getting, and now I'm afraid of losing him. I need your help! How do I keep him interested in me when he has this huge fan club of adoring girls?

—The Green-Eyed Girlfriend

I was like, Just great ☹! My advice about the Brady cupcake thing had totally BACKFIRED!

And to make matters worse, my Miss Know-It-All letters were starting to pile up.

That's when I decided it was time to consult my favourite experts on human behaviour. And I was NOT talking about Dr Phil.

Whenever things got really out of control, I could always count on my two BFFs. . .

Chloe, the self-help guru, and Zoey, professor of chick lit and all things sappy!

I was going to ask them to stay after school next Tuesday to read over my letters and give me advice on how to answer them.

If anyone could help me sort out this mess, THEY could!

☺!!

Dear Miss Know-It-All,

I am thirteen and originally from Boise, Idaho.
I just transferred to this school last term,
and I already hate it. My experience with the
people here so far has been terrible. On my
first day, at lunch I sat at a table of girls
who seemed to be fun and outgoing. I thought
maybe they wouldn't mind me sitting with
them. But boy, was I wrong!

When I introduced myself, everyone got
quiet and just stared at me. I felt really
awkward! Then I went to get some napkins,
and when I returned, everyone was snickering.
That's when I discovered my lunch was missing.
It had been tossed in the rubbish along with my
backpack!

I want to go back to my old school in Idaho
or just not go to school at all! What did I
do to deserve this?

—Missing Idaho

Had I been anyone else, this letter would have been challenging to answer. But no one was more qualified to give advice to a troubled and traumatised newbie than me. I knew exactly what to say.

Dear Missing Idaho,

I know being new isn't all sunshine and rainbows. I understand how you feel, because I've been through that experience before, myself. But don't judge everyone so quickly. Not everyone is a mindless clone, and you'll find there are kids who have attended WCD for years who also feel like they don't fit in. Only, these people may not stand out as much because they're quieter and more mature than the loudmouthed, attention-starved "popular" crowd. Hang in there! When I felt like giving up, I finally met my friends. And know that the snots who trashed your lunch are way more insecure than you. Be sure to talk to your parents or a teacher about what happened. And just remember, things will get better!

Your friend,
MISS KNOW-IT-ALL

I wanted to tell her all of my horrific tales about being tortured by the CCP girls and their goblin queen, MacKenzie.

But my letter would be so long, it would end up looking more like a book.

No! It would be a book SERIES!

I hoped my words would give Missing Idaho a little bit of motivation to hang in there and give WCD a chance.

I had a hunch who might have written that letter.

And I planned to keep an eye out for her and invite her to hang out with Chloe, Zoey and me during lunch next week.

☺!!

OMG! OMG! OMG!

I just got a letter that's pretty much freaking me out! I think I know who wrote it. . .

Dear Miss Know-It-All,

I met a girl last September and we immediately hit it off. She's cool, smart, funny and a talented artist. I'm beginning to think we could be good friends or maybe even more. But I'm really bad at expressing myself. And whenever I try to tell her how I feel, I panic and just end up staring at her like an idiot.

My biggest fear is how she'll react because I'm not really sure if she likes me back. I'm also worried she'll find out that I don't come from a wealthy family like all the other kids at this school. I haven't told anyone about that because I'm afraid they'll treat me differently.

Should I be honest with her and risk being rejected or keep everything to myself so we can stay friends?

—Shy Guy

What if Brandon wrote this about ME?! SQUEE!!

OMG!! I just had the most horrible thought! What if Brandon is writing about MacKenzie?!! Maybe he likes her and NOT ME ☹!

Dear Shy Guy,

PLEASE think things through carefully before you tell your friend you like her. It could be the BEST decision you ever made in your life. Or it could lead to immediate doom and despair! It's safe to say that if she is an awkward-yet-adorable shy girl, you have nothing to fear. You should TOTALLY tell her you like her! She probably definitely likes you too! But if you're crushing on a lip-gloss-addicted CCP with a personality faker than her glue-on eyelashes, I can only say this: DON'T DO IT! She's a mean, selfish SNOB, and you should run away SCREAMING (not that I know her)!

Your friend,
MISS KNOW-IT-ALL

P.S. Gook luck! You're gonna need it!

Okay, I admit my letter was a little biased. But you'll never guess what happened next. Shortly after my advice was published in the newspaper, Brandon actually asked me if I wanted to skip lunch and work on an extra-credit project with him in bio.

And while we worked, we had a serious chat.

BRANDON AND ME, HAVING A REALLY DEEP CONVERSATION WITH EACH OTHER

He said there was a lot of stuff he wanted to share with me about his background, but he was a little nervous about it.

He said he felt SO comfortable around me because I was honest and truthful and comfortable in my own skin (unlike MacKenzie).

And I didn't pretend to be something that I wasn't because I was very secure. He actually said I was an inspiration to him and that he admired me and considered me one of his best friends at WCD.

OMG! I was SO flattered.

But then I started to panic when I realised he was TOTALLY WRONG about me.

I DON'T possess any of those good qualities.

As a matter of fact, Brandon doesn't really know the REAL me at all.

But it isn't HIS fault.

I am just the BIGGEST PHONEY at WCD. Maybe even bigger than MacKenzie!

After that conversation, I am SUPERworried about our friendship.

I am so NOT who he thinks I am.

But I REALLY, REALLY want to be that girl because he totally deserves to have a friend like her.

I'm just WAY too insecure and afraid he won't like the very dorky person that Nikki Maxwell really is.

Why is my life SO complicated?!

☹!!

SATURDAY, JANUARY 25

Brandon's birthday is next Friday!

I've checked out all the hottest styles in *Copycat Couture* magazine and have selected the supercute outfit I plan to rock at his party.

I even went the extra mile and started gargling with that teeth-whitening mouthwash stuff every day! Even though it tastes like bleach and stings my tongue. *Copycat Couture* says guys are real suckers for that "I've just been to the dentist" look.

I've put a lot of time and energy into preparing for Brandon's big day. But there's one tiny thing I totally forgot about:

His birthday present! DUH! What was I thinking?!

Chloe and Zoey were smart and bought their gifts for Brandon weeks ago. Fortunately, they offered to go with me to the mall today to help me shop.

Unfortunately, Brianna was tagging along. And she was DYING to go to the grand opening of the mall's Kandy Kingdom play area.

"So, where should we start?" Chloe asked as we stared at the mall directory.

"There's a cool gadget store upstairs. Maybe we'll find something there," I suggested.

Chloe, Zoey and I walked toward the escalator, but I only heard two pairs of snow boots scuffling behind me, not three.

I turned around and saw Brianna standing six metres behind us, frowning with her lips poked out.

"Move it, Brianna! You're slowing us down!" I yelled.

"I wanna go to Kandy Kingdom! NOW!" She pouted.

I knew she wasn't going to move from that spot unless I gave in.

"Fine! We'll go, but we can only stay there for fifteen minutes," I said. "Now, where is this place?"

"We gotta take the Gumdrop Express!" Brianna exclaimed, pointing to a kid-size rainbow-coloured train choo-chooing down the hall. The driver was an old guy in a conductor getup.

"Are you kidding me?" I cringed. "There's no way we're riding that! What if someone sees us?"

"But just look at how cute it is!" Chloe squealed. "It'll be fun!"

"Can we ride it? PLEEEAAASE?" Brianna begged.

225

She and Chloe both made sad puppy eyes at me.

Getting tag-teamed like that was NOT fair!

"All right, already!" I groaned. "Just please stop doing that thing with your eyes! It creeps me out!"

The $90 in my purse was my entire life savings, and that dumb train was $5 per person. Even so, I figured $70 was more than enough for a nice present for Brandon (and ME, too!).

Zoey and I reluctantly squeezed into the back of the small train.

OMG! We were SO embarrassed.

We even covered our faces with our scarves so no one would recognise us.

Meanwhile, Chloe and Brianna sat up front, waving to bystanders and chatting with the conductor the entire ride to Kandy Kingdom.

After we finished the train ride and visited Kandy Kingdom, Brianna started to complain that she was hungry.

"I'm starving! I want Queasy Cheesy!" she whined.

I was annoyed, but I've seen her tantrums when she's hungry. They can get really UGLY really fast!

I had to feed the little monster, so I spent another $19, plus a tip.

After that, we went to the electronics store and Chloe and Zoey helped me find an MP3 player and some video games Brandon might like.

I planned to come back for his gift after we'd visited a few more stores.

However, we hadn't got far when we spotted a pair of really cute and sassy boots in the window of a swanky department store.

OMG! They were HOT!

SQUEE!

Even though we were supposed to be shopping for Brandon, we figured it wouldn't hurt to go inside to take a closer look.

While my BFFs and I were drooling over those boots, I suddenly discovered that Brianna must have got bored and wandered off or something.

Luckily, I spotted her pigtails in the cosmetics department across the aisle.

Brianna was sitting in a fancy chair in front of a mirror, applying makeup and humming to herself.

"Brianna, WHAT are you doing?!" I scolded. "You shouldn't be playing in that stuff. Besides, you're WAY too young for makeup."

Then she turned away from the mirror, looked at me and smiled.

OMG! I thought my eyes were going to actually rupture and bleed!

That pint-size Glamazon had glittery electric-blue eye shadow all the way up to her eyebrows, way too much blush on her cheeks and purple lipstick smeared around her mouth.

She batted her false eyelashes at me. Which, BTW, were crooked and hanging off her eyelids like skinny caterpillars.

"Don't I look beautiful, DAH-LING?" she purred, and posed like a model.

← BRIANNA'S MAKEOVER

I could think of several words to describe her makeup, but "beautiful" wasn't one of them.

"Sorry, Brianna! But you look like a cross between Miss Piggy and a zombie! Now put those makeup samples back where you found them! And clean your face so you won't scare the other shoppers. Or I'll have to put a bag over your head!"

"Meanie!" she muttered under her breath, and stuck her tongue out at me.

When I saw her shove a tube of lipstick back into its brand-new packaging, I almost had a heart attack.

"OMG! Brianna!" I yelled as I sorted through the small pile of the makeup she'd opened and used. "These AREN'T samples!"

"Um, what are samples?" Brianna asked, blinking mindlessly with her lopsided lashes.

"Don't you understand?!" I cried. "We have to PAY for all of this stuff! Otherwise, you'd be stealing!"

So there went the rest of my money for Brandon's gift!

ME, USING PRETTY MUCH ALL OF MY
CASH TO PAY THE SALESCLERK FOR THE
MAKEUP BRIANNA OPENED

I ended up spending almost ALL of it. I had a whopping three dollars and ten cents left!

And we had to spend that on makeup-remover tissues to wash the gunk off Brianna's face. Thank goodness Chloe and Zoey were there to help me clean her up. They're the best friends ever.

But now that I'm flat broke, how am I going to buy Brandon a gift?

There's just no way I'm going to show up at his party with no present. That would be SO tacky.

Maybe I should just tell him the truth. I can't attend because I'm suffering from a severe case of BFS, also known as . . . Brianna Fatigue Syndrome!

Why, why, why was I not born an only child?

☹!!

SUNDAY, JANUARY 26

Answering all these Miss Know-It-All letters is starting to get a little exhausting.

So I've been racking my brain trying to come up with a way to get them all done in less than an hour.

I think I've finally come up with the perfect solution. A form letter! Also known as . . .

THE MISS KNOW-IT-ALL
QUICK-PICK ADVICE FORM LETTER

Dear: _____,
(INSERT NAME)

Reading your very
- ■ sad letter
- ☐ disturbing letter
- ☐ crazy letter
- ☐ freaky letter

was so touching that it actually
- ☒ made me cry like a baby.
- ☐ scared the snot out of me.
- ☐ made me laugh so hard, I cried.
- ☐ made me so sick, I vomited.

I was once in a similar situation when I
- ☐ tried on my grandma's false teeth
- ☒ stepped on a poopy nappy
- ☐ ate an entire box of doggie snacks
- ☐ realised my breath smelled like liver and onions

and seriously thought about just giving up.

I realise that this problem is overwhelming, and you probably feel so
- ☐ nauseous   ☐ angry
- ☒ afraid   ☐ confused

that you want to
- ☐ dye your hair purple.
- ☒ eat a plate of fried worms.
- ☐ mud wrestle a very large pig.
- ☐ shove a hot dog up your nose.

Anyway, after careful thought and consideration about the issue you're having with
- ☒ your crush
- ☐ your parents
- ☐ your best friend
- ☐ your neighbour's dog

I feel the best advice would be for you to
- ☐ run away screaming.
- ☐ join the circus.
- ☒ take a relaxing bubble bath.
- ☐ get a new family.

This should help relieve the

- ☐ humiliation
- ☑ desperation
- ☐ aggravation
- ☐ constipation

you have been experiencing.

Just remember that no matter how

- ☑ gloomy
- ☐ smelly
- ☐ itchy
- ☐ rotten

things are right now, it always gets better.

I hope that this advice was helpful.

Your friend,

MISS KNOW-IT-ALL

Okay, I admit it STILL needs a little more work before I start sending it out to students.

But this will definitely save me a lot of time.

Am I not BRILLIANT?!!

ME, USING ALL OF THE TIME I SAVED ON ADVICE LETTERS TO PLAY GAMES ON MY PHONE!!

I had a bad case of indigestion, and it wasn't from those microwavable wing-ding thingies I'd munched on a few hours ago.

I was having second thoughts about this whole newspaper thing.

My advice column requires me to write dozens of essay-length letters to my troubled and tormented peers, giving them sound, unbiased and intelligent advice.

The thought of ME being Miss Know-It-All is still HILARIOUS.

Hey, I'm the last person I'D ever want to take advice from!

I'd been sitting at my desk, staring at the huge pile of letters to Miss Know-It-All for so long my butt was actually numb. . .

ME, SITTING THERE STARING AT MY HUGE
PILE OF LETTERS FOR SO LONG THAT MY
BUTT WAS NUMB

I didn't know where to begin!

"Why is this so hard?" I groaned, and covered my
face with my hands.

I had no idea how I could be SO exhausted from doing nothing. But I was.

That's when I thought I heard a giggle behind me. But when I turned around, no one was there.

All of the stress and lack of sleep was obviously making me delirious.

When I turned back to my laptop, I was a little freaked out to see two scribbled-on eyes, a crooked mouth and a hand all up in my face.

"HI!!! I'm Miss Penelope, and I can't find my snow boots! I think I left them in here!" Brianna said in a high, squeaky voice that could have shattered glass.

"Don't EVER sneak up on me like that!" I snapped. "You almost scared the wing-dings out of me!"

But Brianna and Miss Penelope both just smiled and stared at me like very evil mannequins or something. . .

BRIANNA AND MISS PENELOPE NEARLY
SCARE THE WING-DINGS OUT OF ME!

"Have you completely lost it, Brianna? Miss Penelope
doesn't even have FEET!"

"Does TOO!" she said, and stuck her tongue out at me.

"Just get lost, already! And tell Miss Penelope to STOP leaving her invisible junk in my room!"

I don't think Brianna heard a word I said. Her very short attention span was already diverted to my computer screen.

"Whatcha writing?" she asked.

"Stuff for the school newspaper," I muttered. "Now, why don't you both go outside and play in traffic."

"Ooh! You're a newspaper writer guy?!" Brianna gushed, obviously impressed. "I wanna be one too! Can I write something? Pretty please!"

"Believe me, Brianna, I'd love to give all this work to you, but I don't want to get fired," I said. "Besides, you're just a kid. The only thing you know about a newspaper is where to find the funny pages."

"Nuh-uh! I know lots of stuff about a newspaper!" Brianna said, giving me a dirty look. "If you won't let me write, Miss Penelope and I will make our OWN newspaper!"

"Fine," I said. "You two can do whatever you want. Just stop bugging me so I can try and get my work done."

"You're gonna be sorry! We'll show YOU who the best newspaper writer guy is!" Brianna fumed.

Then she and Miss Penelope stormed out of my room.

Ugh! . . . Did I just make things worse? I wondered. When Brianna is bent on doing something, she usually makes my life miserable until she gets her way.

After another hour of writing (and barely finishing three letters), I went down to the kitchen for another snack.

"Paper! Get your paper here! Hot off the press!" Brianna shouted, walking into the kitchen with Dad's newsboy cap on and a stack of spiral notebook pages under her arm. "Anyone want a newspaper?"

I rolled my eyes. "By 'anyone' you mean me, right?"

"Oh! I didn't see you there, ma'am," Brianna said, staying in character. "Care for a paper? You can keep up with all the latest news and gossip about the Maxwell family. And I'm giving it away to my next customer for absolutely FREE!"

"Okay." I humoured her. "I guess I'll take one of your newspapers if it's free."

"And guess what, Nikki? Me and Miss Penelope's newspaper is A LOT better than YOURS!" Brianna bragged shamelessly.

Then she proudly handed me a copy.

I hated to admit it, but Brianna was right. Other than Brandon's excellent photography, most of the WCD newspaper is beyond CRUDDY.

Brianna's little "newspaper" was called the *Some Times* and was written in crayon.

"Brianna! Don't you mean to call it the *Sun-Times*, like that famous Chicago newspaper? You spelled it wrong."

"Nuh-uh!" she answered. "It's called the *SOME TIMES!* Because some times it's GOOD news! And some times it's BAD news!"

Okay. You ask a silly question, you get a silly answer.

Brianna's handwriting was so sloppy! I could barely read the first headline:

PRESIDENT PENELOPE PASSES NEW LAW FOR ICE CREAM BEFORE DINNER!

Yeah, right!

I smirked to myself. Not if Mom has anything to say about it.

I was slightly impressed that Brianna had actually illustrated her lead news story. Very CUTE!!

Then I read the headline on the next page:

BIG HAIRY GRIZZLY BEAR WITH STINKY
BREATH FOUND IN NIKKI'S ROOM!!!

Next to the article, there was a picture of an angry, cross-eyed bear with jagged teeth and stink fumes coming out of its mouth.

And it was wearing a light blue warm-up suit that looked just like the one I had on!! NOT so cute!!

"What is this?" I cried angrily. "Why is there a crazy grizzly bear in my room, Brianna? AND WHY IS IT DRESSED LIKE ME?!"

"OOPS! I forgot that was in there," Brianna giggled nervously. "Gee, look at the time! Gotta finish my paper route. BYE!"

She dashed out of the kitchen and up the stairs.

"Hey! You better come back here, or the big, hairy grizzly bear's really gonna get ugly!" I yelled, chasing Brianna to her room.

Lucky for her, she locked her door just before I got there.

I was so mad at that little goofball in barrettes. She was about to experience an episode of *When Animals Attack!* up close and personal!

Brianna's been in her bedroom awhile, so I can only imagine she's up to no good and probably working on the next issue of that tacky piece of rubbish she calls the *Some Times*.

ARGH!! Sometimes I really want to strangle that girl!

But now that I think about it . . .

I wonder if Brianna would be interested in a newspaper job working for the *Miss Know-It-All* advice column.

NOT!

☹!!

TUESDAY, JANUARY 28

It took me FOREVER to finish all my letters for my advice column.

I was SO happy when I finally posted the final one for editorial review. And as usual, my column created quite a buzz.

But by lunchtime all of the help boxes were running over. AGAIN!

To try and control the overflow of letters in the hallways, the school secretary took a large cardboard box, scrawled the words "Mail for Miss Know-It-All", and set it right outside the office door.

It was mind-blowing. By the end of the day I had a box full of 216 letters.

I was SO happy that Chloe and Zoey agreed to stay after school and help me sort and answer them all. I don't know what I would do without them!

This is us BEFORE answering the letters.

MAIL FOR
MISS KNOW-IT-ALL

This is us AFTER answering the letters.

MAIL FOR
MISS KNOW

But the most exciting news today came from Mr Zimmerman himself.

Just as we were finishing up, Lauren rushed in to tell me that Mr Zimmerman wanted to see me ASAP. Although I was finally starting to get used to him, he still made me SUPERnervous.

I didn't have the slightest idea why he wanted to talk to me. Unless MacKenzie was stirring up some kind of trouble.

Maybe she had finally submitted that article about the Great Toilet Paper Caper with all of those lies about her house being egged.

OMG! What if Mr Zimmerman gives the article to our principal? And the principal calls our parents?!

Chloe, Zoey, Brandon, and I could get kicked out of school ☺!!

My heart started pounding, and I broke into a cold

sweat. I knocked on Zimmerman's door, and he asked me to come in.

"Thanks for stopping by, Nikki. Please have a seat. I must admit, I was really shocked and surprised when I heard about what you'd done. And Lauren tells me you had two of your friends helping you."

"I'm really sorry, Mr Zimmerman. It's not as bad as it seems. I can explain!"

"Young lady, there's no logical or reasonable explanation for what you've done! Not only is your advice column the most popular thing in our newspaper, but it's increased our readership by 42%! I KNEW you had it in you! Congratulations, Sparky!"

I just stared at Zimmerman with my mouth dangling open. "Um, that IS great news, actually. Thanks!"

Then the weirdest thing happened. Zimmerman's eyes started to tear up a bit as he held up a large certificate with a red ribbon around it.

"Each month I select an MVP from the newspaper staff. It's my pleasure to award this certificate to you based on your outstanding contribution to the WCD newspaper as the advice columnist Miss Know-It-All. May you live long and prosper, Sparky!"

MR ZIMMERMAN PRESENTS ME WITH A
CERTIFICATE FOR MVP OF THE MONTH!

OMG! I was SOOOO happy!

But more than anything I was relieved.

Me and my friends weren't in trouble after all.

And now Miss Know-It-All is an award-winning columnist!

EAT YOUR HEART OUT, MACKENZIE!!

There was even more good news.

Because I was getting swamped with letters, Mr Zimmerman suggested that I select and answer only six to eight letters a day, just like a real syndicated advice columnist. EASY PEASY!!

So now I no longer have to kill myself trying to answer two hundred letters a day. WOO-HOO!

☺!!

WEDNESDAY, JANUARY 29

I should be asleep right now. But unfortunately, I'm wide awake, trying NOT to freak out!

I knew I should have just waited and checked my help boxes after school like I always do. But I didn't have time today because I STILL needed to get Brandon a birthday present.

That's when I decided to request a hall pass from geometry class. Since the hallways were usually totally empty during class hours, I could gather my letters and keep my identity a secret.

I had made my rounds around the school and had only one box to go.

I crept up to it like a ninja, and in a flash, snatched off the top and stuck my hand inside to grab my letters.

But that's when I ran into a major unexpected complication. Namely . . .

MACKENZIE CATCHES ME TAKING LETTERS
OUT OF MY HELP BOX!

"Nikki, WHAT are you doing?! Aren't you supposed to be in the toilet?"

"Um . . . I was on my way there right now, actually.

But it's none of your business. Who do you think you are? The TOILET POLICE?!"

"Well, who do you think YOU are? Miss Know-It-All? I'm sure she wouldn't appreciate you snooping around in her letters like—"

That's when MacKenzie stopped midsentence and stared at me VERY suspiciously.

"Wait a minute! Are YOU Miss Know-It-All?!"

"No way! I wrote a letter to her because I need her advice. I was just putting it inside the box."

"So why is the top off and your hand inside? Couldn't you just drop it through the slot?"

"Actually, I had to take the top off because . . . you know, um . . . the little slot thingy was . . . clogged up."

MacKenzie looked at the top. "The slot doesn't look clogged to me."

"Of course it doesn't! I just UNCLOGGED it. DUH!"

I slammed the top back on the box and glared at MacKenzie.

Then we both walked back to class.

But get this! She started staring at me really evil-like and whispering to Jessica.

And everyone knows Jessica is the biggest gossip in our school.

Since she works in the office, she gets all the juicy inside information straight from the teachers and staff.

I actually think Jessica must have blabbed to MacKenzie about Mr Zimmerman naming me MVP of the month or something.

Because when I saw her at my locker after class, she was SO mad, fire was practically shooting out of her ears.

262

Personally, I think MacKenzie is just SUPERjealous because:

1. Brandon's party is in two days and she STILL doesn't have an invitation.

2. She suspects I'm Miss Know-It-All, and MY advice column is way more popular than HER very LAME fashion column.

3. Zimmerman gave ME the MVP award.

4. Brandon and I are becoming really good friends.

I just knew that girl was going to say something to me by the way she was looking me up and down like that.

And boy, was I right.

She slammed her locker shut and suddenly got all up in my face like acne cream or something.

I just looked at that girl like she was crazy. . .

LISTEN, NIKKI! I'M SICK AND TIRED OF YOUR LITTLE MIND GAMES!

MACKENZIE, GETTING ALL UP IN MY FACE FOR NO REASON!

"Jessica tells me Zimmerman gave you a little award. Congratulations! But I wouldn't get too comfortable around here if I were you. I have a meeting with Principal Winston tomorrow morning about a little toilet paper incident. Personally, I think the three perpetrators deserve a permanent suspension."

"It's about time you FINALLY figured out it was me, Chloe, and Zoey and NOT Brandon," I said.

"Are you kidding? I'm NOT stupid! I knew it was you guys all along. I was watching you clowns through my bedroom window the entire time."

"You actually saw us?! Then why didn't you try and stop us before we toilet-papered your house?!"

"Why would I want to interrupt your little shenanigans? Especially when I could use it against you guys to get you thrown out of this school? Like I'm going to do tomorrow!"

"So, why did you blame it all on Brandon if you knew it was us all along?" I asked.

"I knew he wouldn't want me to get you and your

little friends in trouble. And I was going to keep you out of it as long as he played along and agreed to hang out with me and invite me to his party. Everyone says we'd make such a CUTE couple! But he wasn't interested. Guys are fickle like that!"

MacKenzie was using ME to try to manipulate HIM into a relationship. AGAIN! But I totally trusted Brandon and knew he was a true friend.

"MacKenzie, you're a sick little cookie! I can't believe you're playing all of these mind games just to get an invitation to a party!"

"You say that like it's a bad thing! Anyway, I can hardly wait for you to leave so my BFF, Jessica, can move in to your locker. When Winston kicks your butt out of here, we'll FINALLY be rid of the very foul stench in this hallway."

I just stared into her beady little eyes and didn't say a word.

I'd been through SO much drama trying to stay

at WCD. And NOW I was about to get kicked out because of the Great Toilet Paper Caper?! A harmless prank! That MacKenzie had milked for all it was worth.

But more than anything, I felt really bad for Chloe and Zoey. They were getting dragged into this mess only because MacKenzie was trying to hurt ME!

I knew I needed to find my BFFs and warn them, but right then I just felt exhausted and overwhelmed.

The past month has been one wild roller-coaster ride. And it was about to come to an end. As it derailed, crashed and crushed all of my hopes and dreams into tiny pieces.

Later that night I had the most awful nightmares one after another.

But only ONE of them was horrible enough to actually wake me up. . .

After MacKenzie talks to Principal Winston tomorrow, I'm pretty sure I'm going to get in really big trouble. And maybe even kicked out of school.

If that happens, not even my bug extermination scholarship can help me stay at WCD.

And to make matters worse, when my parents find out about all of this, they're going to KILL ME!!

All I can do right now is bury my head in my pillow and have a really good cry.

My situation is HOPELESS!

I GIVE UP!

☹!!

When you're waiting for something HORRIBLE to happen, time seems to slow down. Which means the school day drags on and on and on.

I am so exhausted I can barely keep my eyes open. That's because I was up most of the night either crying or having nightmares.

My life feels so out of control.

Right now I'm supposed to be in the janitor's closet getting a refill for that hand sanitizer thingy in the library.

But I've been so stressed out all day that I need to write in my diary really, really bad.

If I don't take time to vent about what just happened, I feel like I'm going to . . .

EXPLODE!!

I've been a nervous wreck all day, wondering if MacKenzie was actually going to carry out her threat and report us for the Great Toilet Paper Caper.

Since it was getting towards the end of the school day, I started thinking she was just playing more mind games. Maybe she had decided NOT to go through with it after all.

But sure enough, while we were shelving library books, the office secretary sent down three passes for Chloe, Zoey and me to meet with Principal Winston right away.

I SO wished we hadn't toilet-papered MacKenzie's house like that. Now we were going to have to suffer the consequences.

Chloe, Zoey and I hung our heads as we silently walked down the hall to the office. It felt like we were going to our executions or something.

The worst part was not knowing whether our

parents had been contacted or whether they were going to be there at the meeting.

When we entered the office, the secretary smiled and asked us to have a seat right outside the principal's office.

"I have to run a quick errand," she said, "but I'll be back in a few minutes. Principal Winston is still on the telephone, and as soon as he gets done, he'll meet with the four of you."

Four of us?! That's when we turned around and saw MacKenzie sitting there staring at us with her beady little eyes.

We took a seat right across from her.

Then we tried our best to ignore that girl.

OMG! We were so SCARED it was pathetic.

But MacKenzie just sat there with this little smirk on her face.

I think she was enjoying watching us squirm.

Talk about AWKWARD!! . . .

CHLOE, ZOEY AND I WAIT
NERVOUSLY FOR OUR EXECUTION!

But more than anything, I wanted to slap that little smirk right off her face. And I seriously thought about doing it too.

Hey! If it was left up to MacKenzie, Winston was going to give us the worst possible punishment, like being kicked out of school.

So by slapping her silly, what did I have to lose? I'd just be expelled for TWO things instead of ONE. But I decided NOT to do it.

Suddenly the door opened and Marcy rushed in.

"OMG! I can't believe I have all of you together!" she gasped. "Mr Zimmerman wants me to do an investigative reporting piece on a controversy at school. I heard through one of my sources about an incident that happened between you guys a few weeks ago."

"YOU DID?!" the four of us responded, and blinked in surprise.

"Yes, and it's unbelievable! This story is breaking news and will be on the front page tomorrow. I'm hoping it's going to get picked up by the local press, and maybe even AP national. MacKenzie, I'm here to interview you and get YOUR side of the story."

This was NOT good news for us.

"You want to interview ME?!" MacKenzie asked as she smiled, batted her lashes and slathered on five layers of Wretched Revenge Red lip gloss.

Then, being the drama queen that she is, she sniffed and dabbed at fake tears. "OMG! It was just so . . . so . . . traumatising! But I'm willing to share my very tragic story with the entire world. So, Marcy, why don't you, um . . . call Brandon so he can get a close-up photo of my pure anguish?"

That's when I threw up in my mouth a little. Chloe and Zoey just rolled their eyes. That girl was SO full of RUBBISH her breath smelled like the city dump!

"Do you mind if I tape this interview?" Marcy asked. "I'd like to have a permanent record."

"Sure!" MacKenzie answered.

"That'd be great!" Marcy said. "Now let's get started. . . . MacKenzie, I heard from a VERY reputable source that not only did you STEAL Nikki, Chloe and Zoey's costumes for the *Holiday on Ice* charity event, but you LOCKED the girls in a dark storage closet at the arena as well. What is your response to this allegation?!"

MARCY INTERVIEWS MACKENZIE!

OMG! At first Chloe, Zoey and I just stared in shock.

Then we couldn't stop snickering.

MacKenzie looked like she'd seen a ghost or something.

But the funniest part was that her lips were moving but there was no sound coming out. Probably because she knew that every word she said was going to be recorded.

That's when Principal Winston finally opened the door to his office. "Good afternoon, girls. Come right in. I believe you requested this meeting, Miss Hollister?"

MacKenzie looked at Principal Winston and us. And then she looked at Marcy.

We looked at MacKenzie and Principal Winston. Then we looked at Marcy too.

Marcy looked at Principal Winston and MacKenzie. Then she looked at us.

Only, I could have sworn she winked.

All of this looking at each other went on for what seemed like FOREVER!

Suddenly MacKenzie cleared her throat.

"Actually, Principal Winston, I just wanted to have a little meeting to . . . you know . . . ask you about . . . um, the. . ." She looked around the office nervously and spotted an apple on the secretary's desk. ". . . the APPLES . . . in the . . . cafeteria. We really need more apple stuff! Like apple dumplings, apple pie, applesauce, apple turnover, apple . . . um, everything!" MacKenzie said nervously.

I couldn't help but imagine her standing there like an airhead with a huge tray of apple snacks. . .

AN APPLE SNACK FOR YOU, AND AN APPLE SNACK FOR YOU! EVERYONE GETS AN APPLE SNACK!

"Don't you agree, Nikki?" MacKenzie asked, and batted her eyelashes all innocentlike.

I shrugged. "No, not really."

I was NOT about to bail her out of this one.

Principal Winston looked highly annoyed and scratched

his head. "Miss Hollister, you actually requested this meeting to discuss adding more apples to the cafeteria menu?"

"Um, yes! Apples . . . ROCK!" MacKenzie said, and smiled really big.

"Well, okay then. I'll mention your idea to the head cook. Now, if you girls don't have any other pressing matters to discuss, I do have quite a bit of work I need to tackle," Mr Winston said, glancing at his watch.

"There's nothing else I want to discuss," MacKenzie rambled on, "and I'm pretty sure there's nothing else my good friends here want to discuss either. Right, girls?!"

We all just folded our arms and gave her a dirty look.

Then she continued. "Thank you for your time, Principal Winston. Now you get right back to work. We know you're busy, busy, busy! And we're all going back to class. Right, girls?! And we're going to study, study, study!"

Just like that, our meeting with Principal Winston was over even before it got started.

When we finally got back to the library, we did a group hug! Only this time it included Marcy. . .

↑
MARCY

OMG! Chloe, Zoey and I were SO relieved that fiasco was OVER.

We thought for sure our parents were going to be called in and we were going to get expelled from school or worse.

We couldn't thank Marcy enough for helping us out of that big mess.

"You guys are the only friends I have here," she said shyly.

"Well, we consider YOU a friend too!" I said.

"Unequivocally!" Zoey said.

"Absolutely!" Chloe added, and gave her jazz hands.

That's when my curiosity got the best of me.

"Actually, Marcy, what I really want to know is this: HOW did you find out about MacKenzie stealing our costumes and locking us in that storage locker?"

"Every investigative reporter has their secret sources. And mine is a SUPERreliable one!"

Then she held up a very familiar newspaper. . .

We cracked up laughing.

Apparently, Brianna has been handing out her *Some Times* newspaper to kids in her class. And Marcy's little brother had brought one home.

I could NOT believe Brianna was actually putting all of our personal family business in the streets like that. But thank goodness she had.

Another strange thing was the timing of Marcy's interview with MacKenzie. PERFECT!

"I was in the girls' toilets and overheard MacKenzie bragging to Jessica that she had scheduled a meeting with Winston to get you guys kicked out of school," Marcy explained. "MacKenzie also said she was pretty sure your dad was going to close his business to come work full-time for HER dad. And as soon as he did, she was going to convince her dad to transfer him to the other side of the state just to get rid of you."

I felt like I'd just been hit in the face with a bat.

So that was the master plan!

If my dad stopped working for WCD, I would lose my scholarship. But to make sure I was permanently out of her hair, MacKenzie was going to convince her dad to transfer my dad to the other side of the state?!

Which meant we'd have to move.

And if he refused to move, he'd end up UNEMPLOYED! After he'd pretty much liquidated his own successful business and sacrificed the WCD scholarship he'd arranged for his daughter.

I felt SO SORRY for my dad! He probably had no idea he was dealing with such RUTHLESS people.

That's when I noticed all three girls staring at me.

"Nikki, are you okay?" Zoey asked. "You don't look so good."

"Actually, I DON'T feel very good. I think it was

that leftover Casserole Surprise we had in the cafeteria," I lied.

I could NOT believe I had gone through ALL of this drama for the past month only to find out in the end that I might STILL have to leave WCD!!

I blinked back my tears.

Then I prayed my dad WASN'T planning to quit his job to work for MacKenzie's dad full-time.

But after he'd got rid of his van last week, the likelihood of that happening seemed very high.

At least things had turned out okay for Chloe and Zoey.

But the thought of having to say goodbye to them and Brandon was just . . . heart wrenching!

They say "Life is like a box of chocolates".

But my box is full of the yucky, gooey, smushed, cherry ones!

And that STINKS!!

!!

OMG! OMG! OMG!

All I can say right now is . . . OMG! I don't even know where to BEGIN!!! My day was just so . . . OMG!!

Even though I didn't get expelled from school yesterday, everything was still pretty much a disaster.

I knew that as long as my dad was working for MacKenzie's father, my life was going to be a major DRAMA FEST!

Brianna and Miss Penelope woke me up by jumping in my bed and screaming, "Wake up! Wake up! Dad has a really fabulous surprise for us. Come outside and see it!"

I was like, JUST GREAT ☹! He was probably going to announce he'd taken that job with MacKenzie's dad and we were moving. There was probably a huge moving van parked outside or something.

I quickly put on a sweater over my pj's and trudged out into the cold morning air. Brianna was right! It was a FABULOUS surprise. . .

DAD, MAX THE ROACH, AND OUR RAGGEDY OLD VAN WERE BACK WHERE THEY BELONGED!

I never thought I'd be so happy to see all three of them together again.

Dad explained that although he liked working for Hollister Holdings, he preferred being his own boss. And he liked having a flexible work schedule so he could spend more time with his family.

He said working for Mr Hollister had inspired him to try and expand his OWN business, Maxwell's Bug Extermination.

That's when Mom told Dad that he had proved to both her and the world that he was a shrewd and savage business shark after all.

We were all so proud of my dad that we tackled him and gave him a big hug and a kiss.

So it looks like my bug extermination scholarship won't be in jeopardy after all.

MacKenzie's going to blow a gasket when she finds out.

She is such a control freak!

But at least she's not controlling my dad anymore.

Anyway, later this evening when I was getting ready for Brandon's party, I found out at the last minute my mom had to stand in for a sick parent and be the driver for Brianna's dance class car pool.

Mom was all like, "Nikki, dear, I'm STILL planning to take you to Brandon's party. But we have a teeny-tiny complication regarding your transportation HOME. So your dad has agreed to help."

I could not believe my own mother would LIE right to my face like that. Sorry, Mom! But it WASN'T a teeny-tiny complication.

IT WAS A SUPERSIZED, GIGANTIC, HUMONGOUS BLOB OF A PROBLEM!!

WHY?

Because my parents casually informed me that I was going to be picked up by—wait for it, wait for it . . .

DAD and Max the Roach.

Even though I was happy Dad was no longer working for Hollister Holdings, there was just NO WAY I was going to let Brandon see me getting into that wacky-looking roachmobile.

And even worse, he finally would know what a huge PHONEY I am.

Why couldn't DAD drive for Brianna's dance class?!

Then, instead of brutally traumatising ME for LIFE, Dad could take Brianna and her little friends joyriding. It would be more fun than DISNEY WORLD!!

BRIANNA AND HER FRIENDS, JOYRIDING IN THE ROACHMOBILE

That's when I made a VERY difficult decision. I was NOT going to Brandon's party ☹! Even though I had a present for him, after getting this week's allowance.

And being the honest person that I am, I planned to tell Brandon and all my friends the truth: Something had come up at the last minute.

Namely, my LUNCH! I was so SICK of my life ☹!!

I had picked up the phone to break the bad news to Chloe and Zoey when my mom knocked on my bedroom door and stuck her head inside.

"Nikki, dear, would you please write down the time you need to be picked up from your party along with the address and telephone number and give it to your dad? He doesn't have the best memory and gets lost going to the mailbox."

But before I could tell her I'd changed my mind about the whole party thing, she closed my door and disappeared into the hall.

I just sighed and dialled Zoey's number.

Actually, Dad NOT finding the house would be a really GOOD thing because—

Suddenly a little lightbulb clicked on in my brain, and I had a stroke of pure genius.

Brandon's party was going to be at Theo's house because he had a cool, arcade-style games room with an awesome sound system. The address was 725 Hidden Lake Drive. But what if Dad parked and waited for me somewhere else? At ANOTHER address? Then no one at the party would see me getting into the van with him and Max the Roach.

PROBLEM. SOLVED. ☺!!

I quickly hung up the phone.

Then I scribbled all of my party information for Dad.

Just like Mom had instructed.

Except I kind of fudged on the address-and-phone-number part:

PICK UP NIKKI
AT 10:00 PM

710 HIDDEN

LAKE DRIVE

TELEPHONE:
555-0129

Was I not brilliant? ☺!!

Anyway, Brandon's birthday party was just as fun as
I had imagined.

It was really cool hanging out with all my friends.

I even surprised myself and had a total change of heart about ~~asking~~ begging Brandon for that extra invitation for someone to attend his party, namely . . .

MARCY

Sorry, MacKenzie and Jessica ☺!!

Chloe and Zoey kept me laughing.

And as usual, Violet brought her fab music collection and rocked the house.

Literally!

Theo had just about every type of pizza imaginable delivered hot and fresh by Queasy Cheesy.

Yep — Queasy Cheesy!

I was shocked to find out that Theo's family owns the one at the mall. As well as the other 173 locations in the national chain.

And get this!

As a special treat, his dad gave each one of us three FREE gift certificates for an all-you-can-eat Queasy Cheesy Pizza Fest.

OMG! I was SUPERhappy about that!

Because if I gave one Queasy Cheesy certificate to Mom, one to Dad and one to Brianna, I'd pretty much have ALL of my Christmas shopping done for next year!

Without having to spend ANY of my OWN money.

How COOL is THAT?

Anyway, I couldn't believe how quickly the time passed, and soon it was 10:00 p.m.

But we were having so much fun, no one wanted to leave.

I wasn't really the least bit worried because, according to my brilliant plan, my dad was patiently waiting for me somewhere nearby.

So of course I had a complete MELTDOWN when the doorbell rang and . . .

MY DAD HAD JUST
CRASHED MY PARTY!!
AAAAAAAAAAHH!!!!

The GOOD news (if you want to call it that) was
that my situation was so MASSIVELY HORRIBLE
that it COULDN'T possibly get any WORSE!

Or so I thought.

Theo's dad, Mr Swagmire, scratched his head and
looked even more confused than my dad. "Hmm?
Now, that's strange! All of the houses on this street
are 720 or above. But you're welcome to use our
phone to try to reach your daughter. Come in and
make yourself at home."

"Thank you. I appreciate your help. One quick
phone call should clear all of this up. . ." said my
dad.

That's when I decided it would probably be a good idea to grab the phone BEFORE my dad did.

But not to keep him from using it. I needed to call 911 to report a brutal crime that was about to occur.

Because when my dad finally figured out that he was wandering around LOST, on a cold, dark night, all because I'd given him a bunch of PHONEY information, he was going to KILL ME!!

The night had turned into a complete DISASTER!

My FRIENDS were down the hall.

My CRUSH, Brandon, was standing next to me.

My DAD was at the front door.

MAX THE ROACH was parked at the curb.

And I, NIKKI MAXWELL, was about to PEE my pants!

MAP OF THEO'S HOUSE

DECK

LIVING ROOM

ENTERTAINMENT ROOM

MY FRIENDS

MY CRUSH →

STAIRS

FOYER

KITCHEN

OFFICE

MY DAD

GARAGE

ME (FREAKING OUT)

VAN →

When Dad walked over to the phone to call me, I was so close I could have reached around the corner and touched him.

But I just stood there frantically holding my breath.

I was DOOMED! And any second now I was going to be SO BUSTED!

Or maybe . . . NOT.

I was SUPERrelieved when Theo came over and dragged Brandon away to show him his new video game system.

Just as Dad began dialling the phoney number, I spotted a telephone across the hall in the kitchen that was, luckily, out of his view.

I knew it was a crazy idea. But what did I have to lose?! I was already in way over my head.

So I quickly tippy-toed into the kitchen and snatched up the phone just before my dad finished dialling.

"Hi, Nikki! Boy, am I glad to hear your voice. I'm totally LOST! But . . . HOW did you know it was me?"

"Actually, I didn't! Er, I just, um . . . saw the caller ID?"

"That's strange! I'm not calling from home!"

"The caller ID said, um . . . Dad. And you know, it's totally a coincidence that YOUR name is Dad too. Because there are, like, millions of guys out there named Dad. Actually."

"Um, okay. Well, I can't find a house with the address you gave me. And right now I'm calling from a neighbour's house. I need you to find out the correct address."

"Well, Dad, you sound SO close by. Almost like you're in the next room or something. Hey, I bet if I looked out of this window right here by the phone, I just might be able to see—OMG! There it is! Dad! I see your VAN! It's parked about five houses down. Can you believe that? Wow!"

"Really! I guess I was waiting in the right place after all. That means I WASN'T lost!"

"Dad, why did you think you were lost? You just need to drive down the street five more houses. And if you give me a few minutes to say goodbye to everyone and grab my coat, I'll be right out."

"Okay, sweetie. I'll see you in a few minutes, then."

"Bye, Dad! Love you!"

I could NOT believe that our little conversation went so well.

Now, if Dad would just simply

1. hang up the phone

2. walk out of the house

3. get into his van and

4. drive further down the street

I WOULDN'T have to run away from home and join the circus.

I peeked from the kitchen as Dad thanked Mr Swagmire, shook his hand, and finally left.

Mission accomplished ☺!!

But then I turned around, and . . .

WHAT'S UP?
WANT A CHIP?

?!

GULP!!

"Oh! Hi, Brandon!" I sputtered. "I didn't see you standing there. I was . . . on the dad with my phone. Er . . . I mean, on the phone with my dad."

I wondered how long Brandon had been standing there watching and listening.

"Is everything all right?" he asked.

"Yeah, I'm fine. Thankfully, my dad just left. HOME! He was here to pick — I mean — he's COMING to pick me up. . ." I stammered.

Brandon just kind of stared at me suspiciously and slowly nodded his head. "Really? Um, okay."

I could feel my cheeks getting warm and I started to squirm. "Well, I better get going. I don't want to keep my dad waiting."

"But I thought you said he just left home?"

"Er, he did. But he'll be here real soon. He's a superspeedy driver. You know, like those guys in

Formula One. Zooooom! That's my dad. Anyway, thanks for inviting me. Bye!"

"Do you have to go so soon? I just. . ." Brandon looked a little disappointed as his voice trailed off. "Okay, then. Thanks for coming, Nikki."

I turned and walked away as quickly as I could.

But I could almost feel Brandon staring at the back of my neck.

I hugged my BFFs, Chloe and Zoey, said goodbye to everyone, and thanked Theo for hosting such a great party for Brandon at his house.

That's when Marcy thanked me for inviting her.

"Thank YOU! For shutting down MacKenzie!" I laughed.

"No problem! If there's ever anything else I can do to help out, just let me know. I have no social life WHATSOEVER."

That's when a little lightbulb went off in my head.

"Actually, Marcy, there is! My Miss Know-It-All advice column has been keeping me pretty busy. Chloe, Zoey and I have been staying after school to work on them. I'd love for you to help out!"

"OMG! YOU'RE Miss Know-It-All!" Marcy gasped. "And you were right! I DID find some friends at this school."

So now Marcy will be hanging out with us during lunch and after school. She's a good kid!

As I stepped into the cold, crisp night, I felt happy and a little sad at the same time.

It was a blast hanging out with Brandon, and I liked him more than ever. But just when it seemed like sparks were about to fly between us, they abruptly fizzled.

It was quite obvious Brandon suspected something.

And me sneaking off to meet Dad didn't help
things. But I'd just DIE if anyone saw my roach
van. Especially Brandon ☹!

I casually strolled down the pavement.

But once I got past Theo's garden, I took off running towards the van like a madwoman.

When I climbed inside, Dad was still staring at my note and scratching his head.

"Hi, Nikki. It's really weird, but the house numbers around here don't seem to be in order," he mumbled.

"Don't worry about it, Dad," I said, feeling a little guilty I'd just led him on a wild goose chase.

Then he hesitated and looked SUPERanxious.

"So, let's just keep everything that happened tonight our little secret, okay?"

My mouth dropped open as I stared at him in disbelief.

SECRET?! Dad knew?!

But HOW?!

OMG! Had he seen me at Theo's house?!

"Well, if you tell your mom about me not finding the house, I'll never hear the end of it. She's always teasing that I get lost going to the mailbox," he explained.

I breathed a sigh of relief.

"Don't worry, Dad! Your secret is totally safe with me!" I gushed, and gave him a quick hug.

Then I slouched way down into my seat.

Even though it was pitch-dark outside, I didn't want to take a chance on anyone seeing me riding around with Max the Roach.

The fact that I had managed to survive Brandon's birthday party was a MIRACLE! But now I was worried that Brandon suspected something.

But I didn't blame him. I'm such a massive phoney, I wouldn't want to be friends with myself.

I guess I was just sick and tired of all the secrets and lies. I didn't know how much longer I could keep hiding who I really was. . .

The ONLY person in the ENTIRE history of mankind attending school on a stupid BUG EXTERMINATION SCHOLARSHIP!

WHY was my life so hopelessly CRUDDY?!

That's when I got a text message from Brandon: "I LOVE that kooky Crazy Burger hat and the gift certificates! Would you like to help me use them tomorrow for lunch? Please say YES!"

Brandon had just asked me out ☺!! To eat . . . but still! SQUEEEE!!

It wasn't a candlelight dinner at a romantic Italian restaurant, but Crazy Burger had the best gourmet burgers for miles around.

I texted him my answer right away: "YES! Should I meet you there?"

"Sure! But to be honest, I've been wanting to ride in your dad's funky, cool roach van for months!"

I had to read Brandon's text over, like, three times.

Then I totally lost it and burst out laughing.

My dad looked at me like I was INSANE!

All of these months I've been going insane trying to keep who I really am a big secret. And Brandon knew the real ME all along!

Only, I don't think he knows that I know about HIM!

Or DOES he??!!

All of the excitement and drama and unanswered questions about what we SECRETLY know and don't know about each other is enough to make my head spin.

Just thinking about it makes me feel a little nauseous. But in a really GOOD way!

And yes! I know I sound KA-RAY-ZEE!

But I can't help it.

I'M SUCH A DORK!!!

Hey, you!

Wanna take a sneak peek at a few pages of my next diary, *Holiday Heartbreak?*

Shhhh! It's a secret. . . .

SATURDAY, FEBRUARY 1

OMG! I'm suffering from the worst case of CRUSH-ITIS ever!

This morning I had these fluttery butterflies in my stomach that were making me feel SUPERnauseous ☹! But in a really GOOD way ☺!

I felt SO insanely happy I could just . . . VOMIT sunshine, rainbows, confetti, glitter and . . . um . . . those yummy little Skittles thingies!

I still can't believe my crush, Brandon, actually texted me last night after I left his birthday party.

And you'll NEVER guess what happened??!!

HE ASKED ME OUT TO CRAZY BURGER!! SQUEEE ☺!!

And yes, I know it's NOT like a real date or anything. But STILL!

I was SO elated, I blasted my FAVE music and danced around my bedroom like a MANIAC. . .

Hey! I was beyond FIERCE! I was an air-guitar-playing, dancing machine!

After dancing in my room for an entire hour, I was so tired I could barely breathe.

That's when I collapsed into a wheezing, sweat-soaked mass of body odour and sheer exhaustion.

GASP!!
COUGH!!
HACK!!

A very *HAPPY* wheezing, sweat-soaked mass of body odour and sheer exhaustion.

ME, WITH A BIG FAT DORKY
SMILE PLASTERED ACROSS MY FACE!!

WHY? Because any minute now, Brandon was going to contact me so we could make plans to hang out at Crazy Burger.

SQUEEEEEE ☺!

So I snuggled into a comfy chair, stared at my phone and waited patiently for his call.

Before I knew it, it was bedtime. I felt like I'd been waiting FOREVER. . . !!

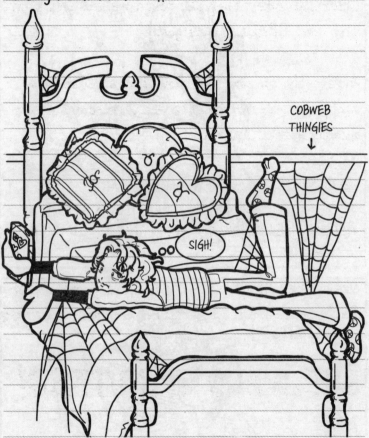

ME, FLOPPED ACROSS MY BED, SULKING

But no call! No email! Not even a text message! I even checked my phone to make sure the battery thingy hadn't run down or something.

Unfortunately, my last call was from my BFFs, Chloe and Zoey. They had called me late last night with some REALLY juicy gossip.

Apparently, someone had showed up at Brandon's party unexpectedly to drop off a present for him shortly after I had left.

You'll NEVER guess who it was!

MACKENZIE ☹!!

Okay, I'll admit it was really nice and sweet of her to do that. But she had totally overlooked one very important little detail . . .

SHE WASN'T INVITED!
☹!!

Which meant MISS THANG had basically CRASHED Brandon's party! Like, WHO does that?!

My BFFs told me that MacKenzie was twirling her

hair, giggling and flirting with Brandon like crazy. Then she got superserious and asked to talk to him PRIVATELY about something really important!

JUST GREAT ☹! Now I'm really starting to ~~worry~~ PANIC!

What if MacKenzie told him some awful lies about me so he wouldn't want to be friends anymore?!!

She's always talking about me behind my back and saying stuff like, "Nikki's a hopelessly insecure, fashion-challenged, diary-obsessed DORK!"

Which is so NOT true! Well . . . maybe it's a little true. Okay! Actually, a LOT true. But STILL!!

WHY did all of this have to happen just when Brandon and I were about to have our very first date-that-really-isn't-a-date ☹?!

PLEASE, PLEASE, PLEASE, PLEASE, PLEASE let Brandon call me tomorrow!!

Don't miss more diaries

Dork Diaries

Dork Diaries:
Party Time

Dork Diaries:
Pop Star

Dork Diaries:
Skating Sensation

Dork Diaries:
Dear Dork

Dork Diaries:
Holiday Heartbreak

by Rachel Renée Russell!

MOST IMPORTANT TIP EVER FROM NIKKI MAXWELL:

Always let your inner **DORK** shine through!

#1 New York Times Bestselling Series

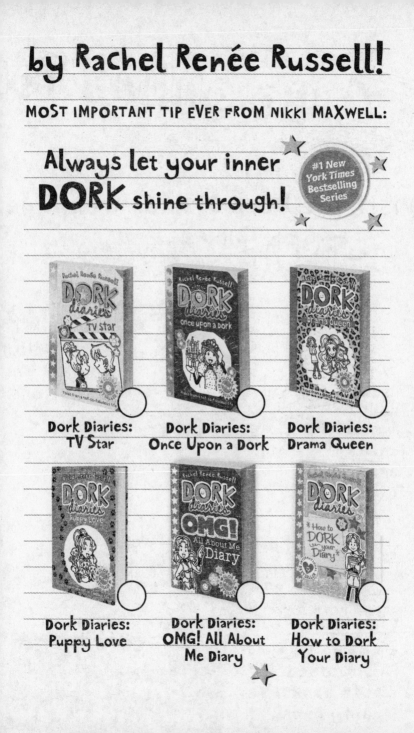

Dork Diaries: TV Star

Dork Diaries: Once Upon a Dork

Dork Diaries: Drama Queen

Dork Diaries: Puppy Love

Dork Diaries: OMG! All About Me Diary

Dork Diaries: How to Dork Your Diary

Go online for

Visit the Dork Diaries webpage:

www.DORKdiaries.co.uk

Read Nikki's secret blog and ask her questions

Submit your own DORK DIARIES fan artwork and videos

"Dork Yourself" widget that lets you create your own Dork cartoon

Exclusive news and gossip!

Download a DORK DIARIES party pack!

Fabulous competitions and giveaways

Do you love

DORK
diaries

and reading all about Nikki's
not-so-fabulous life??

Then don't miss out on the
BRAND NEW series from

Rachel Renée Russell!

featuring new dork on the block,

MAX
CRUMBLY!

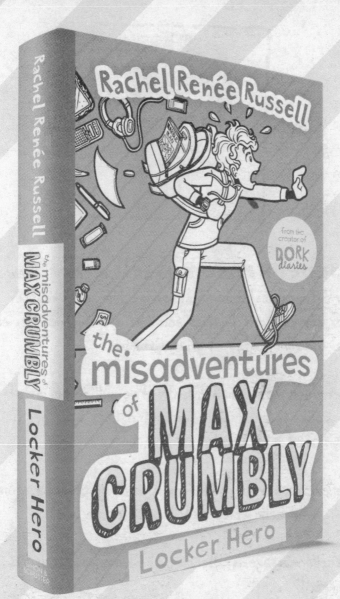

"If you like Tom Gates,
Diary of A Wimpy Kid and, of course,
Dork Diaries you'll love this!" *The Sun*

Rachel Renée Russell is the #1 *New York Times* bestselling author of the block-buster book series *Dork Diaries* and the exciting new series *The Misadventures of Max Crumbly*.

There are more than twenty-five million copies of her books in print worldwide, and they have been translated into thirty-six languages.

She enjoys working with her two daughters, Erin and Nikki, who help write and illustrate her books.

Rachel's message is "Become the hero you've always admired!"

ALSO BY
Rachel Renée Russell

DORK DIARIES

Dork Diaries

Party Time

Pop Star

Skating Sensation

Dear Dork

Holiday Heartbreak

TV Star

Once Upon a Dork

Drama Queen

Puppy Love

How to Dork Your Diary

OMG! All about Me Diary!

Double Dork

Double Dork #2

Double Dork #3

THE MISADVENTURES OF MAX CRUMBLY

Locker Hero

THIS DIARY BELONGS TO:

Nikki J. Maxwell

PRIVATE & CONFIDENTIAL

If found, please return to ME for REWARD!

(NO SNOOPING ALLOWED!!!☹)